ONLY IN
KEY WEST

BOOKS BY
KENNETH D. MICHAELS

THE GAY DETECTIVE
ONLY IN KEY WEST

THE NICK & NORM GAY DETECTIVE SERIES

ONLY IN KEY WEST

KENNETH D. MICHAELS

LA MANCHA PRESS

Published by La Mancha Press

Contact Kenneth Michaels at:
Kenneth.Michaels03@gmail.com
www.kennethdmichaels.com

Cover design by Laura Duffy
Book design by Karen Minster
Author photograph by Carol Tedesco

ISBN 978-0-99832-420-3 (paperback)
ISBN 978-0-99832-421-0 (ebook)

Library of Congress
Control Number: 2016919241

    Michaels, Kenneth D.
    Only In Key West
    (The Nick & Norm Gay Detective Series)

First Edition: May 2017

Printed in the United States of America

FOR

Artists struggling to make
their dreams a reality.

———

All who seek respect, equality,
and acceptance.

———

My parents, Felix and Violet,
sister, Susanna,
and brother, Patrick.

We are more alike, my friends, than we are unalike.

—MAYA ANGELOU

Since it was New Year's Day, Anna knew she could take her time, which was good because she was still getting over a bad head cold. She had been working as a cleaning lady in Key West's city hall for two years and took her job seriously. If she played her cards right, she could stay in America. Anna had her cousin, Vladimir, to thank. Otherwise, she would still be in Moscow. He had *political connections* and pulled some strings to get her hired. She had already learned to speak a little English but was a long way from fluent.

To help pass the time, she put on her earphones and listened to her English lessons, practicing the words. Then she stocked her cleaning trolley and pushed it down the hall to begin her work in the commissioners' area.

First, she unlocked the door of Commissioner Tom Moss's office, then grabbed the handle of the trolley, and backed her way in. She noticed the envelope on the commissioner's mahogany desk, along with a family picture right next to it. The photo had been moved from its usual spot.

Then she turned and saw Commissioner Tom Moss, hanging from the chandelier. She screamed so loud that even the roosters outside the building paused, and it took a lot to get a rooster to stop midstrut.

1

Norm and I arrived in Key West on New Year's Eve at 2:30 p.m. Leaving a twelve-degree, blustery Chicago and landing in a tropical climate of eighty-two degrees made me feel like I had walked into a 3-D version of *Avatar.* The sun was bright and the palm trees danced a tango rhythm to the shifting winds. I could actually smell fresh air.

As we crossed the street to catch a cab, a hen and her brood of six chicks ran ahead of us, while a rooster crowed in the background, warning everyone to step aside for his family.

"What's with the chickens?" Norm asked the cab driver.

"They're our island treasure. Don't hesitate to take some with you when you leave. We've got quite a few to spare." Ten minutes later, he dropped us at our destination, the Hidden Sands Resort.

A picket fence surrounded the two-story, large white mansion that had wild orchids nestled in the trees. The house had two bedrooms, one upstairs and one down, each with two beds and its own en suite bathroom, along with a half bath down the hall. We decided I would take the room on the top floor and Norm would stay downstairs, allowing us both privacy and together time if we wanted.

The house had once belonged to a prominent plastic surgeon, Dr. Harris, who left a lucrative practice in Beverly Hills to become a Parrot Head. I soon learned that every year thousands of Jimmy Buffett fans converged on the island to celebrate the artist and his songs.

Dr. Harris didn't bother waiting for the convention. Instead, he spent nearly every night drinking and singing at Jimmy Buffett's bar, Margaritaville. Since Harris's death, a few years back, his family rented out the mansion to the snowbirds who flocked to Key West for the season. The price was three thousand dollars a week. Hefty by most standards, but the City of Chicago was picking up the tab, our reward for catching The Reaper, a serial killer in Chicago. We had been given a week but decided to stay two, using some of our vacation time.

I had been to Key West before with my late partner, Darren Connor. In the fifteen years Darren and I were together, we visited Key West seven times. It was one of our favorite vacation spots. We always enjoyed watching Sho Yu's descent in the Big Red Shoe, an event as popular as New Year's Eve in Times Square, and one that attracted major TV coverage. She was one of the most renowned drag queens on the island and directed a company of girls in nightly shows at the 801 bar.

Since I had my own TV show, *The Gay Detective*, where I interviewed gay stars, I understood the power of the media. Aside from being a talk-show host, I also worked as a detective in the Chicago Police Department with my partner, Norm Malone. It was difficult to believe that in the last year I had premiered my show, lost my lover, Darren, to a senseless murder, and caught the killer. Not only that: Norm and I nearly lost our lives capturing The Reaper.

What a year!

But that was in the past. This vacation would be turning the page—even if it could never make up for the senseless deaths. Memories of former times in Key West were bittersweet.

Once we were settled into our rooms and unpacked, I told Norm about my plans to watch Sho Yu and hoped he'd join me.

"Do I have to spend my New Year's watching a drag queen waving from a red shoe?" he said.

The local weeklies said they'd been told that Sho had a big surprise for everyone this year. This mildly intrigued Norm, but he wasn't completely sold on it.

"It's not just for gay people, Norm," I said. "It's an event that everyone goes to."

The phone rang. It was Norm's daughter, Patti.

"Hi, sweetheart. Nick is trying to persuade me to go with him to see this queen named after some kind of Japanese seasoning."

"Oh, Sho Yu! She's famous, Dad," I heard Patti say. "Be sure to take some pictures." The deal was done. Norm would do anything for his only daughter.

Sho was indeed famous. The son of an American soldier and a Japanese mother, Sho had lived in Japan until she was fourteen. She came to the States and over the years established herself as the most legendary drag queen in Key West. Much of this was due to the coverage of her popular New Year's Eve event, but she was also known for her kindness and for staging numerous charitable events.

———

THE COUNTDOWN began at ten seconds to midnight. I'd heard from the taxi driver that Sho planned on appearing with her partner of thirteen years, Matt, and making a big announcement once the shoe dropped.

The event had been moved from the main drag of Duval Street to the Outer Mole Pier near Fort Zachary Park to allow for more space, and the area was as packed as an overstuffed blue-cheese martini olive. It was so crammed we couldn't move an inch in any direction, but Norm and I had managed to get there early enough to get a good view. Anticipating the large crowd, the city had allowed Bourbon Street Pub to rent a crane to lower Sho, since the height would make her more visible. There was no doubt that she had staged the whole thing for maximum drama.

"You know I hate crowds," Norm said gruffly, biting his lower lip and puffing out his chest, daring me to defy him. "I'm out of here as soon as this is over and you're buying drinks, kid."

"Sure," I said. *Small price to pay*, I thought.

SHO, DRESSED IN A LOW-CUT white chiffon dress, and Matt, in a black-and-gold lamé tuxedo, waved from the Big Red Shoe. It began a slow descent and then swung over the crowd. Multicolored fireworks brightened and accentuated the night's celebration. The crowd oohed and aahed as the event progressed. Everyone was waiting for Sho to formally announce her marriage to Matt. Close friends knew they had been married at city hall earlier that day.

"Ten, nine, eight, seven," the TV announcer counted. The tension rose along with the roar of the crowd, as the huge sequined shoe descended gradually in midair.

"Six, five, four, three, two…" A slight pause.

But then I heard the grinding sound of metal on metal and the intermittent *SCREECH* of the cable screaming its SOS. Sparks flew off the cable, causing parts of the shoe to catch fire. At first it looked like a dramatic spectacle, but the line had frayed. The shoe wobbled from side to side and picked up speed in its rapid descent. Sho batted away the sparks to avoid becoming a human torch, while Matt tried to protect her by covering her with his body.

Silence blanketed the crowd for a brief moment.

The winch snapped, and the shoe careened uncontrollably, jerking and twisting like a derailed roller coaster until it crashed into the branches of a tree. People screamed and pushed each other, wanting to flee the area, but it was too packed. I could smell the fear of the crowd as the hysteria heightened.

Sho was thrown out of the shoe and fell into the arms of bystanders, including Norm and me. Matt, trapped inside, was not so lucky. When he finally dropped out of the huge shoe stuck in the tree, he looked like a discarded Raggedy Andy doll, his legs twisted awkwardly, with one pointed back at a nearly ninety-degree angle.

He was unresponsive and had numerous cuts and gashes, a few bleeding badly.

I stayed with Sho, who was dazed and mumbling something I couldn't understand, as Norm tried to clear a path to Matt.

"Police, coming through. Make way," Norm shouted, but his voice was lost in the chaos of the crowd. Then he put his fingers in his mouth and gave a loud whistle, catching the group's attention. Norm and I started to create a corridor for the local police force managing crowd control. They were doing everything they could to keep the event from turning into more of a disaster. I spotted a tall, handsome cop in a khaki uniform coming toward us.

"Move the crowd back. Set up a perimeter for the ambulance to get to the scene," commanded the large man, who seemed to be in charge.

Then he turned and looked in my direction and made eye contact. In that brief moment his eyes searched my soul as if testing the waters. Then he smiled. I was embarrassed to feel a powerful shot of testosterone charge through me as intense as a Taser jolt.

Then he walked over and introduced himself.

"Chief Perez," he said, as he shook my hand with a warm but forceful grip. He held my hand for a nanosecond after shaking it.

"Nice to meet you. I'm—"

"Nick Scott, of course, the Gay Detective."

Norm quickly came to my rescue. "Norm Malone, Nick's partner. We came here for a little R and R—"

"And got caught up in the festivities."

"If that's what you call this," Norm said.

"Only in Key West."

"What?" Norm asked, puzzled.

"It's what we locals say. You'll see. After a while, you realize certain things can only happen here."

"Nick, maybe we made the wrong choice."

Chief Perez looked me up and down. "I don't think so. In fact, I'm sure you didn't."

WITHIN MINUTES, we heard the sirens wailing from the fire station, which was only a short distance away.

Sho was trembling and still speaking incoherently as I cradled her in my arms. Her once-perfect makeup was streaked by blood trickling from the cuts she sustained. Norm joined the police in keeping the crowd of rubberneckers from pushing in for cell-phone snapshots of the scene.

The EMTs put Sho and Matt on stretchers and hoisted them into the back of two separate ambulances. I saw a slim guy, wearing tight jeans and a rainbow-colored tutu, slip into the back of Sho's ambulance and wondered who he was. The ambulances took off as fast as they could, their sirens screaming as they raced to the Lower Keys Medical Center emergency room.

2

Chief Perez invited us to join him in his police car. He drove rapidly with his siren on, speeding through the streets, so we arrived at the doors of the emergency room before the ambulances.

Perez jumped out of his car and moved quickly toward a light-brown-skinned man wearing a flowered green surgery cap, a knee-length white medical coat with a stethoscope around his neck, and blue scrubs. He stood in the middle of five other medical personnel at the doors to the emergency room.

"Dr. Mercado," Perez said, shaking his hand warmly. "Glad to see you and your team are working tonight."

"We're ready. What can you tell me?"

"Sho seems dazed. She was shaken up after the fall," I jumped in.

"The other guy is pretty messed up," Norm said. "Bleeding, unresponsive."

Just then one of the ambulances spun around the corner and pulled up to the curb. The two EMTs in the back jumped out, lifted the gurney to the pavement, and quickly rolled Matt through the doors and into the ER.

Perez, Norm, and I hurried in behind Dr. Mercado and his team, heading past the triage desk and down the hall to a treatment room.

"Intubation!" Mercado ordered as Matt was lifted carefully off the gurney and put onto a white-papered table. Someone handed the doctor a flexible plastic tube, but we couldn't see what was happening as several of his assistants crowded around him for a few silent seconds. Then Mercado raised his head and looked at the spectators, smiling, as if he expected applause.

"Success!"

"Can we talk to him now?" Perez asked.

"Did you not see me put a tube down his throat? If and when he gets better, you will need my permission."

It was the first time I saw the chief back down.

We waited for the ambulance carrying Sho, hoping she was now lucid and could tell us what had happened.

Dr. Mercado gave the nurses some instructions and we followed him back out to the curb. In another two minutes the second ambulance pulled up at the door of the ER where we stood.

The driver got out and rushed to the back door to let his partner out.

"Where's Sho?" Perez yelled at him.

"I don't know."

"What!" Perez's face was turning red.

"We had to stop because the ambulance was overheating. We went to check under the hood," the driver said. "And when we got back in, she was gone."

"Where did you stop?" I asked, since Perez's mouth seemed too contorted to speak.

"I don't know, really," the driver mumbled. "It was so dark and there weren't any streetlights on the road."

"Somewhere in the mangroves," the other EMT said.

"Who was with Sho?" I asked.

"She was alone," the EMT answered.

Sounds like money passed hands in this cover-up, I thought.

By this time Chief Perez had recovered some of his composure and began to take charge again.

"All right," he snapped. "That's enough of this bullshit. You guys are coming with me down to the station for questioning. I'll read you your rights when we get there, but if you don't tell me what really happened between the crane crash and pulling up here without Sho, I'll charge both of you with aiding and abetting an attempted murder and lock you up."

Good idea, I thought.

"Can we come along for the ride?" Norm asked.

"How else are you going to get home tonight?" Perez shot back.

I sat in front with Perez, while Norm bulked in between the two cowering suspects in the back of the car as we raced to the police station.

When Chief Perez pulled up at the station, he sat in the front seat with me for a moment and asked me something in a whisper.

"Could you and Detective Malone meet me tomorrow afternoon at Sandy's?"

"Who's Sandy?" I asked, also whispering. I gestured at Norm to lean in closer so he could hear the conversation.

"It's a place, not a who," Perez explained. "A coffee stand attached to the laundry down on Virginia and White Street. I'd like your help on something."

"They starch their eggs?" Norm asked. "That sounds like a weird setup. Food and laundry."

"I like to eat, and why not eat while you're waiting for your clothes to dry?" Perez said. "Sandy's is well known for their coffee and sandwiches."

"Grub and suds," Norm said. "Sounds good to me as long as they don't mix it up."

"What do you need help with?" I asked

"I've got to book these suspects so I can't tell you now. But I want to consult with you two tomorrow. Can you meet me there at three?"

"We'll be there," I said, as Perez got out. I avoided looking at Norm, who I knew wouldn't be pleased to hear I'd promised a meeting on New Year's Day, an afternoon he usually filled with football games.

This was supposed to be a vacation, I could hear him thinking.

"Sergeant Henry," Perez barked at another officer just getting out of his cruiser. "Take these two gentlemen home, please, while I lock up these dirtbags."

3

At 3:00 the next afternoon, Norm and I walked through the open side door of the M & M Laundromat, which also housed Sandy's. The laundromat, usually packed with customers, was deserted and ghost-like; rows of silent washers, dryers, and metal transfer carts piled up in a corner like abandoned dodgem cars. It felt peaceful, unlike my level of jumpiness from the previous night.

I slept poorly due to the iguanas playing tag on the roof. My idea of nature was admiring fresh flowers or a coastline from the eighth floor of a sunlit luxurious boutique hotel. Despite the wildlife, the eighty-degree weather made up for it all.

I threw on a pair of shorts, a T-shirt, and flip-flops and was ready for the day. Norm, however, hated the heat and was wearing khaki pants, a maroon jersey shirt, and orthopedic shoes. He looked like he was going to a meeting of the Rotary Club. I was determined to get him a more fashionable outfit before the day was done.

We had rented a car, and it took us only five minutes to get to Sandy's.

"Over here." We heard Perez's voice at the counter near the window. "I've got steaming hot coffee for all of us." He waved us over.

14

"Good afternoon, Chief," I said as Norm and I sat down.

"Welcome to my other office," he replied.

Perez was wearing white shorts and a Hawaiian shirt open at the collar. He had dimples, a square chin, thick black hair, and looked like he worked out regularly. He wasn't wearing a ring. So far, he was receiving checks in all the right boxes on my personal list.

"What's up?" I asked.

"Let's cut to the chase. The two suspects we booked last night refused to talk. Wouldn't tell us anything about where they took Sho, except that she feared for her life and had to hide. They're sitting in jail waiting for a bail hearing later this morning."

"What do you want us to do?" Norm asked. "And how about some ham and eggs?"

"Listen up. Have either of you big city whizzes heard of Commissioner Tom Moss?"

"Nope," I said.

Norm shook his head.

"This morning the woman who cleans up at city hall found Moss in his office, hanging from a chandelier," Perez said.

"Ugh," Norm said.

Maybe this will spoil his appetite.

Perez continued. "He was a prominent, progressive commissioner and, for the most part, respected by the community."

"So?" Norm was getting really impatient. And hungry. I could tell.

"He left a note. Listen to this."

He reached into his briefcase and pulled on surgical gloves. Then he took out a plastic bag holding a sheet of stationery, which he removed gingerly, and read, " 'So long. Wherever I'm going can't be worse than working with you a-holes. Happy New Year. Moss.' "

"Sounds bitter about something."

"It doesn't sound like him at all. My gut says this is no suicide." Perez sipped his coffee.

"Why is that?"

A minute passed. I looked at him, thinking he was gathering his thoughts, but soon realized he wasn't going to answer me for whatever reason. Maybe he didn't know. Maybe he forgot what he was going to say.

"You wanted to consult with us about how—" I started.

"Right," all business-like again. "I want you to do your thing for both of these cases: Sho's disappearance and her alleged fear of being murdered and the death of Commissioner Tom Moss."

Silence again, all around. I could see Norm had actually stopped thinking about food. Like me, he was a born detective and loved the hunt, the process, the solution to every crime. Both of these cases were interesting. I'm sure he was thinking the same thing I was. We had become soul mates after the nearly fatal investigation last year.

"Okay, Chief Perez, we're supposed to be on a vacation, but there's nothing like a good case. Agreed, Norm?"

"Right. I was getting bored with all the friendly people and good weather."

"Let's start by you telling us everything you know, starting with Sho. Why would she think her life's in danger? Where is she now?"

Perez smiled and waved over a colleague, who had recently pulled up in the parking lot. After introductions, Perez asked him to get us some breakfast. When he'd left, Perez huddled down and began talking in a hushed tone. "The person who knows the most about Sho is Mercado."

"The ER doctor?" Norm asked.

"None other. He and Sho go back a long way. He helped her get settled when she first got here. Some say they were lovers for a while, and maybe still are."

Norm's stomach growled, making me smile, but he was so engrossed, he ignored it.

"Mercado has lived in Key West a long time and is respected. Before coming here, he had a practice in Miami and still commutes there occasionally."

"And?"

"That's all I have."

A brood of chickens came up to the bench where we were sitting, looking for any stray crumbs that may have fallen. Norm and I were surprised to see them so close to us, but Perez ignored them and they moved on, looking for better prospects. Chickens here were as common as pigeons in the Midwest.

"Okay. What about Tom Moss?" Norm asked. "Have you checked out city hall's security cameras?"

"Forensics is on it," Perez said.

"Women problems?"

"Rumor was he was having an affair, yet he claimed to love his family. He was a difficult read."

Norm nodded as if running through a mental checklist.

"Illegal activities?" I asked.

"Most likely. He was a slick guy and knew a lot of sketchy people."

"You ever have any personal problems with him, Chief?"

"Nah."

"Any connection to Sho's accident last night?" I asked.

"None that I can see. Sho didn't like him and neither did Dr. Mercado. Didn't like his style. Moss had his share of enemies."

"It's not always easy to tell when someone's going to take his own life," I added. "Sometimes they seem fine, even happy, right before they do themselves in."

Just then a dark cloud formed and covered us in shadow. A bolt of thunder interrupted the conversation and I was sure we were in for a storm, but within five minutes, the cloud dissipated and the inviting sky was bright blue again. I could smell sizzling bacon from the café.

"What do you think about the note?" Perez asked.

"We need to find out what kind of personal problems might have led him to this," I said.

"Nah," Norm interrupted. "I agree with you, Chief. The guy was murdered, so we need to find out what he was into on the sly and who his enemies might be."

It wasn't like Norm to ignore my take on a case and I wondered why he was so eager to side with the chief. Maybe he was cozying up to him to see where he was taking us.

"Want to go see the body?"

I'd like to see your naked body, I thought, and then dismissed the notion as obscene, realizing how much Darren would have disapproved.

"Dessert?" I asked. "You always this gracious with your guests?"

"Just the ones I like," Perez said.

I smiled. Was that his way of saying he liked me? I didn't want to read anything into it because I was sure my gaydar needed a tune-up, but it still felt good to be around him.

Perez checked in by cell with the detectives on the case and they told him forensics had just finished up at the crime scene and the body had already been taken to the morgue. He looked over at the counter to get the clerk's attention. "We're taking those sandwiches with us. *Vámonos.* Let's go."

I looked over at Norm to confirm he felt okay about taking on this case. We could still back out. He shrugged.

"All right," I said.

I'd have to work on my tan starting tomorrow.

4

The Key West morgue was located in Lower Keys Medical Center at the end of a dimly lit hallway. Unlike Chicago's, Key West's buildings didn't have basements because of hurricanes and subsequent floods. The walls were painted a soulless green and the corridor was flanked with paintings of past officials, whose ghostly images reminded me that regardless of rank or office, this was the last stop.

Perez led the way. He introduced us to the medical examiner, Dr. Perry, a rotund man, cleanly shaven, with a red bloated face lined with broken capillaries around his nose and eyes.

"Welcome, Chief." The ME paused as he looked at me. "Nick Scott? The Gay Detective? I've heard about you."

"And Norm Malone, his partner," Perez chimed in. "We wanted to take a look at Moss."

"Always glad to have a couple of new eyes. This way."

The smell of alcohol filled the air, making my nostrils flare as I braced for the revealing. He led us across the large Mexican-tiled room to a steel table, where Moss was laid out. Layers of fat peeled back from the body left a gaping hole. His stomach was displayed on the table beside him.

"Just looking to see what he'd ingested before death. Might provide a clue."

I noticed bulging eyes and contusions around his neck. I'd seen numerous autopsies in my career, but I never developed the necessary objectivity of seeing a human body dissected like a frog in a biology class. I felt nauseous but was able to keep it at bay, unlike the first time, when as a rookie I had heaved.

"Have you determined cause and time of death?" Perez asked.

"A rope for cause. The angle suggests suicide. As far as time, can't say for sure, but from the body temperature, I'd guess sometime between four and eight this morning."

"Find anything unusual?" Norm asked.

"Just surprised to see him hanging. Didn't seem like someone who'd take his own life. They don't match, but I didn't really know the man."

"Could he have been a gasper?"

"Autoerotic asphyxiation?" Dr. Perry asked. "Doubt it."

"He liked women and partying even though he was married," Perez added.

"You have many suicides last year?" I asked.

"Counting him? Four, plus another five mysterious deaths," Perry said. He looked at the corpse and then at us. He picked up his scalpel and we knew he was finished answering questions.

"If you find anything unusual, will you give me a call?" Perez asked.

"You betcha."

As soon as we got out of the morgue, I tried to broach the subject delicately. "Say, Chief," I began. "I didn't realize there were quite so many suicides and murders lately."

"I didn't want to scare you two away, but it's true. Things haven't been quiet around here for a while now."

"There's got to be a connection," Norm said. "This is no coincidence."

"Right." Chief Perez seemed to be in a hurry. "But I can't talk now." He flashed a killer smile at us. "I'll leave it to you two geniuses to be creative and start sleuthing. But here's a hint. Start at the Bourbon Bar over at 801 Duval Street. You'll love it. Locals just call it the 801."

And with that he was gone.

———

AS WE WALKED BACK into the house, the sun began to set. I felt the hot breeze blow through my hair and saw a large orange-and-black bantam rooster pecking in the grass. He looked up once to check out his new visitors, then quickly returned to his search.

"What do you think?" I asked.

"I think you got a crush on Perez," Norm said.

"I'm talking about the case," I insisted, trying to change the subject. "The humidity is high." I wiped the sweat from my brow. "I'm really hot."

"The chief thinks so, too."

The rooster raised his head and crowed as if supporting Norm.

I slammed the door, upset that my emotions were so transparent to Norm. I thought I had managed to keep them hidden, but we had been through a lot together.

THE NEXT MORNING I got up around 9:00 and swam laps in our backyard pool. It was medium sized with crystal-clear water, surrounded by a deck filled with lounge chairs and potted palms.

Swimming was one of my favorite exercises and after sixteen laps, I felt completely refreshed. I lay out on one of the chairs even though it was early. If I did nothing else, I wanted to come back from this so-called vacation with a tan.

I must have dozed off because I was awakened by Norm's loud voice.

"Ain't this the life, Nick—sun and a pool right in our back-yard?" He then did a cannonball into the pool and splashed water all over me.

I jumped up. "Dammit, Norm. I was drying off."

"So now you can do it again. Life repeats itself, ya know."

I had to smile. His perspective was simple and true.

"Hey, come on in, the water's fine." He splashed around and waved for me to join him.

I wanted to relax, but he wouldn't give up and finally I gave in. We had a water fight and he almost pinned me in a corner but I managed to wriggle free. We were like two kids. After a half hour we were both exhausted and lay by the pool, catching our breath.

"What do you want to do tonight?" I asked him.

"I'm picking up a hot chick, we're going to have a few drinks, and then make some whoopee," he said.

"In other words, nothing."

"Yep."

"How about we start getting to the bottom of this crime spree and make some inquiries about Sho at the 801?"

"We could do that."

With that, he lay back in the chair and in a few moments was sleeping, snoring. I put on my earphones and relaxed.

AFTER A FILLING DINNER and a few drinks at the Reach, I was enjoying a nice buzz. We made our way over to Duval Street in search of the 801. Everyone we asked on the street told us we couldn't miss it.

And they were right. At the intersection of Duval and Petronia Streets, the city had installed permanent rainbow crosswalks to mark the center of the LGBT entertainment district. In front of the pink-stucco 801, a group of drag queens dressed in neon colors stood talking to possible customers.

"Show starts in an hour."

"Don't miss a show you can't get at home."

"Best show on the island."

We got some whistles as we approached, and one of the girls walked up to Norm.

"You look like a hot one. What are you doing later, honey?"

Norm was so embarrassed he didn't know what to say at first and then came back with, "Don't think you could handle me," in his thick Chicago accent.

"I've handled a lot of things. You look like someone who needs some special care. Never underestimate Polly Saturates."

Polly was about six feet tall. Her hair was styled in a short cut and her face was flawless. She wore a slinky silk floral print with a slash up the side to expose her long, shapely legs.

"Where you from, doll?" she asked.

"Chicago."

"Isn't that where Santa's from?"

"He's moved farther north," Norm said.

"Heard he's into chimneys—or was it poles?"

"Don't get naughty." Norm shook his finger at her in warning. "When it comes to that, Santa's tough."

"You sound tough, honey. Just my type, rough trade."

"You can back off anytime," Norm said.

"Is he your lover?" she asked, wedging her way between us so she was looking straight at Norm and blocking me from his view.

"Naw, we just work together."

"I bet you do."

Sin Onhym, a blonde in a low-cut coral blouse, tight black slacks, and orange six-inch stilettos, approached me. She had an angular face and large fake boobs that got even my attention. Being only about five foot five and slender, she was a knockout. Norm couldn't get his eyes off her.

"So if you're not with him, that means you're by yourself," Sin said.

"Yeah, but I'm not looking, either."

"Playing hard to get, huh? Usually the wildest in bed."

They worked in the business and outrageous was their language. They teased and shocked their would-be customers until they hooked them and got them into the club.

"Actually, I wondered if I could ask you a few questions?"

"Ask away."

"Do you know where Sho is?"

The girls went silent. A warning bell had gone off.

Another drag queen walked over and introduced herself as Ora Lee. She wore a bright lime sarong and a tropical top made of silk flowers. She looked like a table centerpiece.

"You're police, we got it. We've already been questioned, so you can forget it."

"Maybe you left a few things out."

"You look familiar. Of course. You're the Gay Detective."

When the other girls heard the phrase, they all stopped talking and flocked over to me.

"I love your show."

"Can you interview me? I'm famous, or will be if you interview me," Ora said.

"This isn't about the show, but thank you."

The girls were less guarded once they realized who I was and what it could mean to their careers. Media and exposure were everything to them. They were in show business and wanted to be the next RuPaul.

"Then what's it about?" Sin asked. "What are you guys doing here?"

"We want to find Sho and keep her safe. We know she's in charge here and were hoping you could help us find her," I said.

"Any idea where she is?" Norm asked.

A chorus of "nopes," "uh-uhs," and "nos" rapidly followed. They were loyal to their boss and we were the fuzz.

"The sooner we find her, the faster we find out who wants to do her in, right?"

"That's the jackpot question, isn't it?" Ora said. "Believe me, if we knew, you'd be the first to know."

"You sure about that?" I asked.

"I don't lie." She giggled. "Well, maybe about a few things, but it's always innocent. Well, maybe not totally innocent." She paused, thinking about what she just said. "Shit, I'd say anything if it got me laid," she finally admitted and gave out a loud, deep laugh.

"Does she have any enemies?" Norm asked.

"Some people considered her an activist because she fought for the underdog, the homeless, the poor. Few people know how many of us she's taken under her wing, even let us live with her."

"Okay, okay. I get it. How's Matt doing?" I asked.

"Better, but he's still critical and in ICU. We rotate sitting with him," Polly answered.

"That's good," I said.

"He's family. We take care of our own." Polly stifled a sob. "Don't make me cry. My makeup."

"Was there any connection with Tom Moss?" I asked.

"Not that I know of," Ora said. "Unfortunately, he can't answer any questions for you." Ora became guarded. I guessed that she and Sho were close, and Ora would never say anything that might harm her friend.

"What about the other suicides and murders going on around here?" Norm asked.

"Hey, you guys are the cops—don't ask us."

"But we're from out of town," I said. "We don't know the whole history. Can you bring us up to date?"

"You ever hear the story of Bum Farto?" Sin said, coming closer.

"Who's Bum Farto?" I asked. "Is that his real name?"

"Fire chief back in the seventies," she responded.

"What happened to him?"

"Some say he swims with the fishes." She smiled.

"Cement boots?" Norm asked.

Sin nodded, turning her lips down in mock sorrow.

"Shut up, Miss Sin," Ora interrupted. "Let me give these guys a little history lesson. Back in seventy-five, eighty-five, and ninety-five, we had what you call Bubba busts."

"Bubba busts?" I asked.

"You know, cronies in cahoots getting caught," Sin explained. "Including politicos."

"Coke and weed were all over the island. You could buy them behind the counter at convenience stores, restaurants. Most of the local police just looked the other way, since they were on the take, but the Feds were watching," Ora continued.

"Damn," I said. "I hate to hear stuff like that."

"The most colorful bust was in seventy-five. But somebody blew the whistle, probably some dealer who got shorted, and next thing we know the FBI raided Bum Farto's office at the fire station, where he had the drugs delivered. Nineteen Key Westers got handcuffed that day."

"Probably ran out of cuffs," Sin added.

"So the press got a hold of it," Ora went on. "The mayor called an emergency session and suspended Bum Farto to keep suspicion away from himself."

"Was this Bum Farto skimming and knocked off by the suppliers?" Norm asked.

"No one knows for sure, but someone had to take the hit. The FBI needed to bring in someone responsible, and Farto was it."

"All we know is one day he drove to Miami in his classic old Thunderbird and no one has heard from him since," Polly added.

"For all we know, he could be living a nice life in Brazil or Argentina with a young Chiquita banana."

Everybody laughed, including me.

"That car was a beauty," Polly said.

"That was his Drug-mobile," Ora said. "He dealt right out of it."

"How do you know that?" I asked.

"My uncle bought from him."

Billy the bartender stepped outside and said, "Ten minutes to showtime, girls."

Like soldiers given a command by their sergeant, the girls stopped hawking tickets and hustled inside. A few who worked the late show stayed to hand out fliers and be available for pictures with tourists.

As they went in, Ora turned and said, "C'mon in and see the show. Our treat."

Norm looked at me and his deep frown creases told me he didn't want to do it. He'd done his job and he was ready to move on.

"That's a great idea. C'mon, Norm. I bet you've never seen a drag show, have you?"

"Nope," he said, "and I plan on keeping it that way."

"They don't bite. Unless you ask them to."

"Cute, but it's still a no."

I could tell he was starting to dig his heels into the sand, but I was determined to get him in there.

"Remember the boxing match? I didn't want to go but I finally did and I enjoyed it. You owe me one."

He was weakening. His shoulders slumped and he looked down at his shoes.

"Fair's fair," I said, appealing to a partner's bond.

"On one condition," he said.

"What's that?"

"That if I feel uncomfortable, we leave."

"Of course. I'd never do anything to make you uncomfortable." I knew that once we got in, we wouldn't leave, because he'd want to prove to me he could take it.

Ora smiled, turned, and walked through the door of the 801 with us at her six-inch pink rhinestone heels.

5

Canola Screams was manning the cash register opposite the bar and made sure no one got through the turnstile without paying. A petite girl with chopsticks in her French twist hairdo, I was sure she wouldn't hesitate to use those chopsticks if anyone tried to mess with her.

"Canola, these are my guests. Comp them."

"Sure, Ora." She waved us in and we followed Ora up the steps and into the cabaret.

Ora looked around, deciding where to seat us. A U-shaped bar filled the middle of the room, barstools hugged the side walls, and cocktail tables occupied the rest of the space in front of the stage.

"Follow me, boys. I'm going to put you in the best seats in the house."

We tagged behind as she led us to one of the tables, stage right. The cabaret was small and had a ninety-nine person occupancy sign on the wall.

It was the first show of the evening, and I could still catch scents of old drinks and stale cigarette smoke. No amount of cleanser or freshener could destroy this permanent bar funk.

Ora said, "Drinks are on me. Sit back and enjoy the show."

As we settled in, Penny Tration, the petite barmaid, wearing black fishnet stockings and a skintight spandex miniskirt, came over to ask for our order. She had a warm smile, a pretty face, and a friendly manner but looked like she was still in high school.

"Nick Scott, the Gay Detective!" she exclaimed. "I love your show. Are you here to audition the girls? I'm on later, if you could wait."

"Thank you, but we're here to see your show. I'll have a margarita."

"And you, sir?"

"A Bud."

"Coming right up." She turned and I noticed her tight butt, accentuated by her outfit.

I looked around, and once my eyes adjusted to the dim lights at the bar, I saw a mass of faces staring in my direction. It was a full house.

"We should interview Ora," I said. "She's known Sho for a long time."

"Think she might want to take her place?" Norm asked.

"Could be motive."

The music from *Cabaret* filled the room and a spotlight centered on the face of the host. She wore white makeup, bright red lipstick, a tuxedo top, and a studded leather jockstrap.

"*Willkommen, bienvenue.* My name is Ora. Welcome for those of you who don't speak cabaret. I speak it well. In fact I've been told I have a professional tongue," Ora continued.

A few titters followed.

"She looks just like Joel Grey," Norm said.

"How many of you out there have never been to a drag show before?"

Almost 75 percent of the audience raised their hands. I noticed Norm was holding on to his Bud as if it were a lifeline.

"A lot of virgins out there. Let me explain. We are entertainers. We want you to have a good time. Our livelihoods depend on tips from you. When we walk into the audience, don't be afraid to hand us a few bills, or if you prefer, you can stick it in our cleavage, or our behinds. Do you understand?"

A few "yeahs" came out from the audience.

"I didn't hear you. Can we try that again? Please let me know you understand."

This time the audience came back with thunderous whistles, clapping, and "Woo hoos." One guy was slamming the table with one of his shoes.

"Now that's what I'm talking about. Thank you."

Ora's plan turned out to be just the opposite of what we expected. We thought she placed us in safe seats where we could just observe, but it turned out that the girls catered to the audience right in front of them. The safe seats were in the back behind the bar. This could be to our advantage. Although we were their guests, we were searching for clues to Sho's disappearance.

"We have a special treat for you tonight," Ora announced. "A talented singer from another club, which shall not be named, has made a surprise visit and will be performing for us this evening. Let's give a great round of applause for the famous, or infamous, Mimi Peters performing 'Bottoms Up.'"

Mimi had been on *American Stars* and was well known in Key West circles for doing a flawless Beyoncé impression. She was dressed in a leopard leotard, tight white top, long gloves, and a brunette wig.

From the minute she stepped on stage, she was pumped. She swayed her butt acrobatically, suggesting more ways of using it than I ever imagined. I could only think she must have tried every one of them.

At the end of her act, she took off her gloves and threw them into the audience, and I couldn't help but notice the scratches on her arms and hands. I tried to point them out to Norm, but it was impossible to talk over the loud music. The girls had captured his attention, and he clapped and whistled along with the rest of the group. They appreciated his enthusiasm but enjoyed his generous tips even more.

"She was the one in the back of the ambulance with Sho after the accident," I tried to yell to Norm. He pushed his ear forward, indicating he couldn't hear me.

Sin followed with a hot rendition of "Touch Me There," punctuated by undulations, pelvic thrusts, and the creative use of a wet finger. Norm looked at me with an "I'll get you for this" stare. I shrugged by way of apology but felt a sense of excitement at exposing him to another side of my world that he had never seen.

When Penny came around again, Norm ordered a double scotch. Wanting to keep up, I ordered another margarita.

Sin then came into the audience, wrapped her arms around Norm, and threw back her head and sang:

I'll do anything for you if you, if you, if you touch me there.

Norm wasn't ready to do that, but he slipped her a ten, which she stuck *there*.

The audience identified with his embarrassment and laughed. Even if we wanted to leave, it would have been impossible to get up in the middle of the performance and slip out. It was a packed house.

"It could be a crime of passion," Norm said. "Jealousy over a former lover. Maybe Sho broke up with someone to be with Matt—"

"Or one of them was cheating on the other," I added, but the music was so loud, we could barely hear each other.

When Penny made her next round of serving drinks I asked, "Is there an intermission?"

"No, the show goes straight through for an hour and then the girls stick around to talk to the customers."

I nodded, knowing I would pay for this later unless something changed drastically.

"Any one of these girls could be responsible for Sho's disappearance," I said.

"It's certainly not for the money," Norm responded, having noticed the few tips.

"Fame, notoriety."

By the third round of drinks, Norm had lost some of his inhibitions and laughed as he slipped a fiver into Penny's cleavage. He then leaned over to me and whispered, "Are those real?"

"Ask her. She'll probably let you find out," I said, thankful for liquid confidence.

Instead, he asked Penny, "Who's in charge of the group now that Sho's gone?"

"Polly. Her assistant."

He gave her another five for the information.

Norm, like many of the straights there, was curious and got caught up in the camp of the drag queens. They enjoyed doing what they did and it showed.

"They sure look real. I bet some of these performers are gals."

When Ora finished her last number, she came right up to Norm, looked him in the eye, and pouted. "Oh, I wish you were my type."

Norm paused and said, "Ya know, on a different day..."

———

IT SEEMED OUR TABLE was getting more attention than many of the others, and it was partially due to my celebrity status. Whether or not the girls thought I was doing *American Stars*, they enjoyed trying to shock us.

After each song, Ora urged the audience to be generous as the girls posed for pics. Although I enjoyed the show, I also observed the bodies of the girls, looking for any signs that might give us a clue to Sho's disappearance, such as track lines, telltale bruises, or injuries. These could be partially covered by makeup, but not completely.

When the show ended an hour later, Norm posed for a picture with Polly on one arm and Ora on the other. I took several shots, so I could tease him about it later. Once we had finished our good-byes and promises of returning, I suggested we get home.

Norm was so high on the show and a few drinks, he wanted to continue to party on Duval, so we stopped for a drink at the Smallest Bar in the World, which only had four barstools and looked like a galley kitchen.

"Did you enjoy it?" I asked him.

"It was okay."

His responses proved otherwise, and he was afraid I'd kid him about it. And I would. "You sure seemed to have a good time."

"When in Rome…"

"I have a pic of two of the girls roaming their arms around you. Can't wait to show it to the guys at the precinct."

"I wouldn't advise that. Let me see." I played keep-away as he tried to get it.

"Which number did you like the best?" I asked as he continued his attempts to get my phone.

"'Touch Me There' was great, but Mimi's 'Bottoms Up' was a showstopper."

"Did you notice anything about Mimi's arms?"

"You mean the scratches?"

Although I thought Norm was too involved in the show to notice them, he was too experienced a detective not to.

"Yup. I wonder where she got those."

"Looks like drugs to me. Must still be plenty of dealers around." Norm was sober again and all business. "Bad guys get nasty when they're crossed."

"Didn't look like track lines to me," I said. "We should find out where each of the girls was from the time of the accident to the following morning.

6

Darren and I were roasting hot dogs around a campfire and as I looked over at him, he smiled and said, "I love you."

I wasn't sure why, but I responded with, "'Bottoms Up.'" My response was lost in the sound of helicopter rotors above us.

"What's that?" he asked.

Before I could respond, a long, slimy octopus tentacle reached down and encircled him tightly around the waist as the chopper rose into the sky. Darren struggled to break free.

"Come back!" I shouted. "Don't leave now."

I chased after him but the chopper kept rising higher and higher until I couldn't see him anymore. I ran as fast as I could, hoping to follow, and I stepped over a cliff and fell, down, down, *DOWN* toward the rocky coast of surf and slippery rocks. I woke in a cold sweat, realizing I was having another nightmare about Darren.

———

MY SHRINK SAID it was my post-traumatic stress disorder and that these dreams could continue for a month, six months, possibly the rest of my life. I had had them several times now and never got used to them. I shook my head, trying to clear my mind of the experience, but it lingered. I got up, peed, and then made my way to the kitchen, realizing it was already seven a.m. I was restless and yet still comatose as I looked around for the coffee and made a pot, knowing caffeine would help. I made my way to the patio overlooking the ocean and settled into one of the comfortable lounge chairs, thinking this trip, although labeled a reward for catching The Reaper, came at a very high price.

Then I remembered the show last night and smiled as I recalled how much fun Norm had had. Memories like that kept me going. If Norm had not rescued me, taken me into his home, and made me part of his family, I'm not sure where I'd be today.

Just then Norm appeared on the patio, holding a steaming cup of coffee. He was still in his boxers and nothing else. He settled into a chair at the table and asked, "You okay?" as he scratched his belly, which was hanging over his shorts. Some guys have goals to develop a six-pack; Norm's was to acquire six spares. He badly needed a shave and his eyes were slits as he tried to adjust to the bright light.

"I'm fine."

"You sure?"

I paused for a moment, wondering if I should unload on him again. Norm always knew when I was upset, and he was a good listener.

"I had another nightmare about Darren last night."

"You want to talk about it?"

"Not really. It's the same ole, same ole. He's there. We're having a great time and then he's gone."

"Sounds like a repeat of what happened to you. From what I know about PTSD, it doesn't disappear that quickly. Some experts believe in talk therapy. Others, meds. Some even believe in revisiting the scene. You've tried all three, and maybe you don't see it as much as I do, but you are making progress."

"I feel my heart's been ripped out of me. Nothing seems to help. I don't call that progress."

"Don't forget how traumatic it was for you. You and Darren had just finished doing your first TV show, and then he was murdered. That's a terrible shock." Norm paused for a minute. "When my wife died, I thought my life was over, Nick. She was my rock. I was sure I was going to lose it altogether, but I got through it and so will you."

"Sometimes I wonder. The dreams and flashbacks tear me up. I wonder if I'll ever be able to trust someone again without fear of losing him."

"Trust me. I'm not going anywhere. And give it time. You've come a long way."

I knew he was right, but that didn't make it easier. Norm was one of the few people who understood me. He put things in perspective and often eased my anxiety.

What I didn't tell him were my thoughts about Chief Perez, which I felt were exacerbating the PTSD symptoms. Although I was attracted to him, I was afraid of taking the next step. He was a cop and I knew the dangers involved in our line of work. Could I allow myself to trust myself or another person when it came to romantic involvement? Could I trust anyone other than Norm?

The house phone rudely interrupted our conversation and we both looked surprised at the intruder, thinking few people even knew we were here.

"Who's that?" Norm asked.

"Beats me," I said, wanting to let it go to voice mail, but it continued for another three rings and Norm finally followed the sound and found the phone inside the house, lodged between the couch pillows.

Caller ID said *Tina Stafford.*

I had followed him into the house, my curiosity getting the best of me.

"Yeah," he answered gruffly. There was a pause. Norm usually gave an unknown caller five seconds before he hung up. He rarely looked at caller ID.

"No, we're not interested," he said.

I decided it must be a telemarketer, which would explain his annoyance.

"Who is it?" I asked.

He pointed the phone closer toward his chin and said, "Someone from a TV station wants to interview us," Norm said.

"Let me take this," I said.

He happily handed the phone over. I took it and turned on the speaker so he could also hear the conversation.

"This is Nick Scott. How can I help you?"

"As I was telling your friend—"

"That was my partner, Norm."

"Yes. Well, my name is Tina Stafford and I host a local TV show, *Keys, Please,* and I wanted to invite you and"—she paused slightly—"was it Norm, to come on my show."

"Yes, it was, but we're here on vacation and we'd rather not."

"I understand," she persisted. "I'm sure the last thing you want to do is get back to a TV studio and be on a set."

"You got that right."

She had a pleasant voice with a trace of a southern accent, possibly Georgia or Alabama, I thought. As she talked, I pegged her for being in her late twenties. I looked around the hallway and saw there were colorful paintings of the Blue Heaven restaurant and one of Sandy's, which made me smile. They were signed by Andy Thurber, a local artist, known for his bright watercolors.

I had no desire to be on a TV show, especially as an out-of-towner in Key West. I was on vacation.

"I'm doing a show on the recent disappearance of Sho and the commissioner's suicide," Tina went on.

Norm went back toward the patio. He had left the situation to me. I knew he had already lost interest, and whatever it was, I would take care of it. We often acted like a long-married couple.

"That's being handled by the police department," I said.

"I know, and Chief Perez has agreed to come on the show. It would make it so much more interesting if you and Norm would join us as guests."

She had just made the pot a lot sweeter by upping the ante. *Chief Perez*, I thought, and smiled to myself. Maybe it wouldn't be that difficult. I'd be able to see the chief again, and I felt my heart beat faster and desire destroyed doubts.

"When?" I asked her.

"I know this is short notice, but you know as a famous TV host how this goes. Whenever there's a hot news story, the one who gets to it first wins."

"And you want to be the winner."

There was a pause on the other end of the line.

"When, Tina?"

"Later this afternoon, at four."

"We just got up. Let me talk to Norm and I'll get back to you."

I took down her number, knowing I had already made my decision. Now I had to break it to Norm.

"No way am I going to go on television while I'm on vacation. And to talk about a case that we have no work-up on. Uh-uh. I'm going to stay on this patio and soak up the sun and take advantage of every minute we got."

A few hours passed and I tried again, creasing my face into a deep frown. "Whaddya say?"

Norm took one look at me and grumbled, "Okay, okay. I'm getting the keys."

At three we pulled up to Key West Television studios, situated at the southern tip of Stock Island, just outside of Key West.

Norm wasn't happy about doing the show, but when it came to a case, he became a professional and we had agreed to be consultants. If this could help break it, then that's what we had to do.

I believed all that too, but there was the added extra of Chief Perez's being there. I knew my buddy was doing this partially for me, but he'd never say that. That was too personal.

7

Usually TV stage sets were much smaller than they looked
and this one was no exception. There was Susie, the camerawoman,
four chairs to accommodate all of us, and a backdrop of a Key West
setting, palm trees swaying on a sandy beach with the ocean in the
background. It was a setting no one could complain about, and I
was learning that it was something I could easily get used to.

Tina was in her late twenties, just as her voice had suggested.
She had long blond hair, worn so that it lay over her right shoulder,
and was drop-dead gorgeous. She had perfect white teeth and a
symmetrical face with bright blue eyes.

She had asked us to be there an hour before so we could discuss
her plan. If necessary, there would be time for the makeup artist to
do a few touch-ups.

We sat in a semicircle with Tina in the middle, Chief Perez to
her right, and Norm and me to her left. Chief Perez was in uniform
and looked professional and taller than I remembered. I guessed
him to be about six one. He sat with his legs spread so that it was
impossible to ignore the prominent package between them. Was

this his normal posture, or was he showing off? Either way, I wasn't going to ask him to change a thing.

At the same time, I knew I had to stop my furtive stares so I could concentrate on the interview. I resorted to a creative version of the Serenity Prayer, one I'm sure hadn't been heard before.

God, give me the serenity not to focus on Perez's bulge.

The courage to realize that there is more to life than sex.

And the wisdom to know this is no time to get a boner.

Susie moved in to do a close-up of Tina's face as the show went live.

"Welcome to our show, *Keys, Please*. I am Tina Stafford, and today we have Chief Perez of the Key West Police Department, Norm Malone, detective of Chicago's First District Central, and Nick Scott, also a detective of the same district and host of his own TV show, *The Gay Detective*.

"As many of you know, we have had some shocking events take place in our beautiful city of Key West recently. First, Sho's accident on New Year's Eve, which resulted in the hospitalization of her new husband, Matt Howard. On the way to the hospital Sho disappeared, and, as of yet, there have been no reports as to her whereabouts.

"Second..." She paused for a moment. "There has been the tragic suicide of Commissioner Tom Moss, who was found hanging in his office early New Year's Day. I have assembled these three professionals to give us some insight and perspective on these events.

"Chief Perez, let me start with you. Have there been any new findings regarding Sho?"

"I am not at liberty to say. It is an ongoing case and we're doing everything to solve this perplexing mystery."

"'Perplexing' is right. Word has it that the winch that controlled the Red Shoe had been tampered with, resulting in Sho's terrible accident. Do you have any comments on that?"

"Not at this time. I will say that it was an unfortunate accident and luckily she wasn't killed. We are doing everything in our power to locate her and hope she has not suffered any harm."

"Detective Malone, you and Detective Scott were there the night of the accident. Can you give me any impressions you have of that evening?"

"It was packed. There were more people than sardines in a can, crushed like an audience trying to escape from a burning movie theater, mobbed like a rock star at a concert, trampled by a stampede of running cattle—"

I couldn't help but smile as Norm got carried away describing the crowd.

Tina soon realized he would have elaborated even more, so she interrupted and said, "Thank you, Detective Malone. I'm sure you've been in many situations with overwhelming crowds. Your descriptions give us an idea of how it must have felt." She paused, then turned toward me.

"Detective Scott, you were there also—"

"Please call me Nick."

"Thank you, Nick. Can you tell me what you saw?"

"As my partner mentioned, it was packed. Everyone was focused on Sho's descent. I must say she looked absolutely beautiful in her white chiffon dress and platinum hair, don't you agree?" I asked.

"Yes, she looked very happy. I'm glad you brought that up," Tina said.

I had learned from some of my own guests during my show that describing details to the listening audience was always good. It gave them a picture of Sho's appearance that night.

I glanced at Perez and saw him nod his head in assent. A fast study, he had caught on that I was helping Tina recover from a loquacious Norm.

"She looked radiant that night," Norm said.

"She was, Norm. And she seemed to be enjoying the height and the swinging of the shoe. I understand that usually she is lowered a short distance from Bourbon Street Pub's roof," I said.

"That's right," Tina added. "But back to the question. Did you notice anything unusual?"

"Norm and I have only been here two days and our definition of unusual and your definition for Key West are probably quite different. Chickens everywhere you walk, people greeting strangers as if they were good friends, and no one seeming to have a care in the world are not usual for us, Tina."

She laughed. "I'm sure you're right, Nick." She paused as if wondering if she should add her next comment, then said, "For those of you wondering, Sho's husband, Matt, is still in ICU and I learned just a few hours ago that his condition is critical. I'm sure your prayers and get-well wishes would be much appreciated." She shook her head and got back on script.

"I'd like to change topics and talk about Commissioner Moss's recent death. Chief Perez, has there been anything to suggest it was not a suicide?"

Perez straightened up in his chair, braced to look important. He looked directly at Tina and said, "Commissioner Moss's suicide is a tragic event. His death is a great loss to the community."

"Yes, that's true and our hearts go out to his wife and family. Do you think there is any connection between Sho's disappearance and the commissioner's suicide?"

Perez looked right into the camera. I snuck a look at his bulge. Time to repeat my Serenity Prayer.

"Since we have not been able to talk to Sho, there is no reason to believe there was any connection. But again, I caution anyone from drawing any conclusions until we get more information on the case. I'd like to use this time to say to your audience that if anyone has seen Sho or knows anything about her whereabouts, please call the Key West Police Department. Everyone is concerned about her safety. And, Sho, if you see this, please call us. Your cooperation in this matter is crucial. We can protect you."

I jumped in. "I'd like to add that Chief Perez has asked Norm and me to be consultants on these cases, and we are both glad to be working with him and the Key West Police Department. I speak for both of us when I say solving a case doesn't happen overnight. When Chief Perez says the investigation is ongoing, he means exactly that. He is not trying to avoid answering, he is telling you the truth. Cases sometimes get solved in a month, if you're lucky, but it can take as long as a year or more to solve a complex or elusive case. We will all work together and with luck will come up with some helpful information before we return to Chicago. It is indeed an honor to be working with someone of such stature."

I saw Perez pull back his neck and sneak a glance at me as if to say, "*What was that all about?*" but he smiled.

"Thank you for those kind words, Nick. I'll send you a check when you're back in Chicago," Perez said and laughed loudly.

I joined in his lame joke, hoping it had gained me a few points in the "I think you're hot" category.

I knew I had piled it on really thick, but he had evaded every one of Tina's questions with standard phrases like "the investigation is ongoing."

People had heard that and similar lines hundreds of times before and wanted to know more. I hoped my chiming in about Perez not being just another talking head, but rather a human being who was concerned about those he served, had helped.

"Nick makes a good point. Too often, you all hear those standard lines because they're true. We wish we could solve the case in forty-eight hours and put the criminal away, but everything takes time and patience. Please allow us both, as we all try to solve these terrible cases," Perez said.

"Thank you, Chief Perez. Our time is up. I'd like to thank you and our guests Norm Malone and Nick Scott for coming on our show today. It has been a genuine pleasure. Until next time, I'm Tina Stafford reporting for *Keys, Please*."

The show was over and Tina thanked us again for taking time to come on her show.

"You did a great job, Tina. You tackled two difficult topics and managed to keep them flowing and relevant," I said.

"Thanks, Nick. That means a lot coming from you." She beamed.

Her producer, Vicki Krist, joined us on the set.

"Thanks for coming today, gentlemen. You took time from your vacation and that means a lot to us. I know it's difficult to get away from jobs like yours. "And Chief, it was an honor to have you on our show. We've been trying to get you on here for some time, and I'm glad you decided to do so with our guests. It made it even more special. She then handed Perez and me envelopes. He opened his and raised his eyebrows.

"Mangia, Mangia?" Perez said.

"It's my favorite," Vicki replied. We had both received $100 gift cards.

"Thank you, Vicki," we said in unison.

"Italian, I love Italian," Norm said.

"Norm, name a food you don't like," I said.

He was speechless. Everyone laughed.

As we walked out of the studio, Perez turned to me. "Thanks for making me look like a concerned person and not a bobblehead back there. I appreciate it. To be honest, I hate these things and often come off sounding stiff as a board. The mayor's been on my case to get out there and do more PR."

Norm nodded. "I know what you mean, Perez. These things wear me out. Nick, of course, enjoys every second of it."

"*The Gay Detective* has taught me a thing or two," I said, trying to stay modest.

We stood outside in the heat. Out of small talk, it was time to wrap it up and go our separate ways.

"I'm finished for the day. Why don't you both come by for cocktails?" Perez asked.

"Naw," Norm said. "I want to go back, grab a beer, and veg by the pool."

"I get it," Perez said. "How about you, Nick?"

"Well, I was planning—"

"Go ahead, Nick. Just think, you'll have me out of your hair for a while."

"You don't have any hair." We all laughed.

What surprised and somewhat scared me was being alone with Perez. This was uncharted territory for me. I had been with Darren for fifteen years. Yet, I was ready to give it a shot.

"Sure. Why not? I'm on vacation."

"Follow me," Perez said.

Gladly, I thought. *I'll have another chance to look at that tempting butt.*

I dropped Norm back at the house. Just as he got to the door, I heard the phone ring. I was glad I didn't have to deal with the call.

8

NICK'S EVENING

Perez owned his own home on Washington Street, a couple of blocks from Higgs Beach. It was in Casa Marina, a posh neighborhood associated with wealth and prestige, and set fifty feet from the street with its own circular driveway.

Since Key West had a small inventory of homes, Perez's was considered a treasure belonging to the privileged class. From the outside, it looked like a Spanish bungalow with terra-cotta roofing and a Mexican-tiled front porch wrapped around the house. The subtle colors of the roof contrasted with the ornate electric blue and orange tiles of the porch, giving me an impression of designed elegance.

"Welcome to my humble abode," Perez said.

"Doesn't appear too humble to me," I said.

Perez laughed. "It's been in the family for a few generations. I was lucky enough to be next in line. Legally, it belongs to my aunt Gina, my father's sister."

"You mean there are family members on waiting lists to get homes?"

"Oh yeah. Housing's a problem in Key West, especially if you don't know anyone."

But not if you're the chief of police, I thought. *With rank comes privilege. I wondered if the opposite was true. With privilege comes rank. Nepotism often existed in politics.*

"Would you like the grand tour?"

"Absolutely."

"Drink?"

"Sure."

"Name your poison."

"What are you having?"

"Vodka martini on the rocks."

"I'll have the same."

"You're easy," he said, giving me a lascivious grin. I smiled, not knowing how to respond. "Have a seat." He pointed in the direction of the couch.

It felt good to finally relax and I gave out a loud sigh.

"That sounded anticlimactic."

I liked his corny sense of humor with a flirtatious edge. He made the drinks using Beluga Russian vodka and brought mine to me.

I caught the suggestive tone and toasted, "To us." He grinned.

What the hell am I doing? I thought. *I hardly know this guy and I'm flirting back.* He raised his left hand to caress my cheek and came closer, trying to kiss me. I instinctively moved back. I was a bundle of nerves. He ignored the rejection but backed away.

I was torn between desire and professionalism and wondered if he saw me as the Catch of the Day. I never faced the problem of getting involved with coworkers in Chicago because it had never been an issue.

Unruffled, he slipped off his holster, hung it behind the bar, and said, "I'll be right back. Just need to get out of this outfit. I have an extra bathing suit if you'd like to join me for a swim in the pool in back."

"You have a pool?"

"Sure. It's right through the kitchen. Walk around, make yourself at home."

Not his first rodeo; definitely not the first one in this house. But he was single. Why shouldn't he feel comfortable in his own home? I found myself feeling intoxicated by his confidence and the luxury of his surroundings.

His artistic tastes were eclectic. There were watercolors and large, colorful oil abstracts in the attractive light-turquoise living room. A plush coral couch with two matching retro chairs circled a coffee table. He kept the pastel-yellow kitchen simple, since the large blue-pearl quartz countertop and stainless steel appliances reflecting the afternoon light made the whole room sparkle. The house was immaculate and looked like it was being shown to sell rather than lived in regularly.

I opened the ceiling-to-floor sliding glass doors that led from the living room to the pool outside and I felt as if I had entered a garden featured in *Architectural Digest*. Nearest to the patio door were four dark bamboo chaise longues with contrasting bright blue and green pillows and a matching outside table canopied by an oversized chartreuse umbrella. The yard sprawled outward and deep, with towering bamboo stalks in back. Colorful pots of hibiscus, jasmine, and gardenia were strategically placed throughout the greenery.

I stood transfixed by the crystal-clear pool that shimmered in the setting sun, offering glimpses of the painted mural of sea nymphs and mermaids on the walls beneath the water's surface. An eight-foot fountain inspired by Michelangelo's *David*, spouting water from his mouth and penis, stood at the head of the pool. I took a slow sip of my drink and shook my head when I tasted the strong vodka. Another one of these and I'd be on my back like a spouting David, only it wouldn't be water. Perez did say he was putting on his bathing suit, which meant I'd see a lot more of his body and his bulge. I took another sip of my drink. It wasn't so bad the second time around. *Was I purposely trying to lose my inhibitions so I could be seduced? What would it feel like to be naked in his arms?*

I jumped when he snuck up from behind, wrapped his arms around me, and pushed against me. I enjoyed his body against mine for a few moments, letting the pleasure flow through me. When I turned around, I couldn't help but notice he was wearing only a towel and he was in full salute. The surprise of it caused me to take a small step back.

"I like to swim in the nude, but I brought you a suit."

I smiled as he moved in to kiss me.

I backed away again, but this time less quickly. My reflexes were thwarted by his throbbing crotch against me and the few gulps of vodka inside me.

"I don't think this is professional, Chief," I tried.

"Call me Raphael."

I nodded.

"Would you prefer I put my uniform back on?"

"I didn't say that. It's just that I don't, I haven't, I'm not—"

"Shhh. Relax."

He leaned forward to try to kiss me again, but instead of backing off, I simply turned my mouth away and his lips met my cheek. I nuzzled his neck to feign intimacy. David, at the head of the pool, seemed to be smiling.

Kissing him seemed too personal, but I had enjoyed having his body against mine. He moved closer and removed my shirt, pulling it over my head, so that we could be front-to-front. He was hairy, muscled, and inked with tribal tattoos on both arms, which emphasized the size of his biceps. A shiver went through me as he pulled me closer to him. He took my hand and led me to a couch next to David, and this time I did not resist. I hadn't had sex in over a year, and it felt good to have someone who looked like a Greek god wanting me. This is what I fantasized about, wasn't it? Yes, but it was all new to me. I hadn't thought about having sex at all since Darren's death. It seemed so unimportant.

His hands began to roam over my body, touching me tenderly. I moaned with pleasure. Just as he was about to reach into my shorts, an image of an angry Darren popped into my head.

I felt guilty, as if I were cheating on him. Darren was gone. My feelings were unwarranted, but that didn't change my physical reaction. My erection immediately subsided, and Raphael looked at me in confusion.

"What's wrong?"

"I'm sorry. I can't. I don't want to be a tease. I'm just not ready," I said, as I quickly stood up, smoothed down my shorts, and looked for my top.

"That's not what your body's saying."

He was right. Another few minutes and I would have been his.

"Is it because of Darren?" He knew about my past and had enough insight to ask the right question. He was sensitive enough not to push himself on me. I nodded and slipped on my shirt.

"I should go, Raphael."

I was trying not to sound cold, but it was the only way I could distance myself from him right now. I felt I had already gone too far and was starting to beat myself up. I was a master at that, but at the same time knew it was unhealthy.

There was a slight pause as if he were trying to decide what to say after being thrown into a figurative cold shower.

"Sure. Whatever you want." He seemed disappointed, but not angry.

He quickly threw on a shirt and shorts and walked me to my car. There was no exchange of hugs. I drove home in silence, overcome with guilt.

9

PANDORA'S BOX

I walked into the house and didn't see Norm, and then I heard him splashing around in the pool. I took a moment to collect myself, made a vodka and tonic, and went outside. Norm was drifting on a water raft as the sun began to descend into the horizon. It was six thirty and it was still eighty-one degrees.

"You back already?"

"Yeah." I wasn't ready to talk about it.

"Nothing new about the case?" he tried.

"Nope," I answered. "We didn't get very far," I said.

A polygraph would have shown otherwise, since I felt like I had committed adultery.

Norm was aware I was upset and left it alone. He knew that if I wanted to talk about something I would. He was giving me space and I appreciated it.

"Did you make yourself a stiff drink?" he asked.

"Yeah. Why?" I was sure he was referring to my unsuccessful sexcapade.

"Your mother called."

"So. That's not new."

I had started cleaning up the mess on the patio. I threw Norm's empty beer cans in the recycling, picked up his dishes, and started to go to the kitchen for some paper towels and glass cleaner. Whenever I was upset, my OCD kicked in.

"She's on her way down here."

"What?" I stopped my routine and tried to comprehend the gravity of his statement.

"Your mother, Wanda, is coming to Key West. She's already on the plane."

"Why?"

I ran into the kitchen, got the cleaning supplies, and returned within seconds.

This was major. I squirted the tables and cleaned them in Olympic time.

"You tell me. I certainly didn't invite her. I know better."

I took a big swallow of my drink as I made a quick descent into an unpleasant reality. This was the last thing I needed. For once, I thought I would be able to enjoy myself without my mother around. Why would she want to come down here? My body tensed, and I felt the beginning throb of a migraine.

"When?"

"I have no idea. I don't even know what airport she called from. All she said was she was on her way and then she hung up."

"I'm not ready for this. Not at all. I hope you don't mind entertaining her because I don't want to be around when she arrives. I'm afraid I'm not going to be very welcoming."

I turned the dishwasher on and grabbed a Lysol wipe for the stovetop.

"Then disappear for a while."

I felt a twinge of guilt leaving Norm to entertain my mother, but I knew they got along.

I finished my drink and decided to go out. Not only did I screw up any chance I had with Raphael, but now my mother was going to be all over my business. I needed to escape.

"I'll see you later," I said, and stormed out of the house, heading for 2¢, a bar that I heard was fun and out of the way.

"Be careful," I heard Norm say.

Careful was not what I craved. I wanted to find a bar and forget my problems. I was walking so fast that I nearly walked by the 801.

Some girls were outside and Sin was the first to notice me. She was talking up a tourist but paused a moment to say, "Hey, Nick," before she returned to her work.

"Be sure to catch our show. It's the best on the island and something you'll still talk about once you get home."

Once she finished, she walked over, hugged me, and gave me an air kiss so she could keep her makeup intact. I was sure it took her at least an hour to apply it.

Today, she was wearing a coral-blue silk dress with such a low back that it came dangerously close to exposing the crack of her butt. Sho was such a skilled seamstress that she knew how to make her girls look sexy even if they weren't. It was all about the tease.

I had opened Pandora's box of sexual temptations. Sin looked hot. I had never been attracted to drag queens before and was even afraid of my own thoughts because of my recent experience with Raphael. I felt tainted and thought I projected an aura that said, "I am a sex tease."

Is that what I was? Look what I'd just done to Raphael. If someone had done that to me, I'd be pissed. It had been so long since

I'd dated or even tried to find someone that I wasn't even sure what the rules were anymore.

My shrink would say, *Stop feeling so guilty. You weren't ready and that's that. Either he understood that or he didn't. And if he didn't, he isn't worth thinking about.*

That was the right answer but it didn't make me feel any better. I went inside and ordered a drink, just as Ora came hurrying into the bar, still in her street clothes and without her makeup on.

I thought back to when Norm and I had caught the show. All the girls were expected to start their shifts by encouraging customers in the front of the club.

Ora was running late now.

Inside, there were only five other people spread around the bar. Each seemed to be lost in his own world, drowning himself in alcohol. I wasn't alone.

"Can I get you a drink, Ora?"

"Sure. I'm so late, what does it matter?"

It sounded like she was also in an I-don't-give-a-shit mood. I ordered drinks for both of us, thinking she'd spend some time talking, but she threw hers back and said, "I better get ready. Want to watch a drag queen put on her makeup?"

"Sure."

"We can shoot the shit while I get ready. I'd like the company."

The dressing room was tiny, about eight feet deep and three feet wide. It felt claustrophobic. There were mirrors attached to one wall and costumes and wigs of all colors from pink to Goth black on Styrofoam heads in the partitions alongside the costumes.

"You can sit in that corner over there in case anyone else needs space. You'll be out of the way."

I grabbed my seat. Ora quickly shed her clothes down to her black panties, and then sat at her station right next to me.

"Nick, I like you."

"Thanks, Ora. I like you, too."

At this point, I was attracted to any guy who was decent looking and had most of his clothes off. Alcohol can do that. I had at least four drinks in me, and my inhibitions had melted away with each one. Ora had a nice, well-toned body. Nearly six feet tall, she was lean, 175 pounds. I couldn't help but notice her full lips.

"I think we have a connection."

I gazed at her in her panties and she leaned over and kissed me. It was a peck, but I didn't want to be a tease this time, and as difficult as it was, I allowed her to linger. She reached over, placed her hand on mine, and moved closer. I begin to feel panicky. Just when I thought it might go farther, she pulled away and said, "This will have to wait until later. I have to get ready for the show." I was relieved the decision to stop was hers, not mine. She turned back to the mirror and got to work putting on her foundation.

Even all the alcohol didn't mask the guilt I felt. No matter how hard I tried, I couldn't forget Darren.

I watched in awe as I saw her transform from a good-looking guy to a gorgeous queen.

"Where's your partner?" Ora asked.

"At home."

"So you're out on the town by yourself?"

She had started another layer of makeup with the confidence of an engineer creating the monument of her lifetime.

"Something bothering you, Nick?"

I didn't say anything at first because I was too embarrassed to tell her the truth.

"Nick, talk to me."

"I just found out my mother is on her way here to visit. I'm not even sure where she's staying. We only have two bedrooms."

"Oh boy. Not good."

"It's not that I don't love her. I just need some time away from her, if you know what I mean."

She nodded. "I moved three thousand miles away to get away from mine."

She took out a makeup sponge and evened out her face, not one line or freckle showing. She looked flawless.

"Mine didn't talk to me for four years after I left. She disowned me at first."

"Mine isn't like that. She wants me to be available to her all the time."

We weren't having a conversation. We were talking past each other, like two drunks at a bar.

"In New York, I hustled to stay alive. It was a rough time for me until I met Sho. She became my best friend, but then she moved here soon after."

"Um."

Next, she did her eyes. She took an eyebrow pencil and made her eyebrows look full and just a bit arched. She used liner to accentuate the lids.

"She talked me into leaving New York. I flew here and she took me in. If it hadn't been for her, I could be dead. We started doing drag together, appearing at various clubs, and we've remained best friends ever since. I'm not sure where I'd be if it weren't for her."

"She sounds like a great person," I said.

As Ora continued to talk, she finished her face by attaching super-long eyelashes that looked big enough to fan the stuffy dressing room. Her face took thirty minutes total.

"Sho's amazing. I'm just one story out of many. You have no idea how many of us she's helped. I miss her. I wish she were back here."

Next she put on her bra, squeezed herself into a tight sequined pink sheath, and added a matching neon wig. Her talking never ceased and I wondered if she was on something.

"Nick, can you make sure my wig is combed out in back?"

"Sure."

As I got up to help her, she backed into me and pressed her butt into my crotch, holding it there for about a minute so that I forgot all about her wig. Instead, I nestled my nose into her neck, put my arms around her, and pulled her against me, but then she backed away again. As we played sexual ping-pong, I wondered which one of us was more confused. I realized I wasn't the only tease in the room. Ora had it down to a science, could even teach a course to PhD candidates.

"If one of the girls, even from other clubs, is having a hard time, we'll donate the night's tips to her," she said, as if nothing had just happened.

"Just last week, Madame Ovary from Aqua down the street came down with pneumonia and couldn't pay her rent. We dedicated a show just to her and were able to collect enough to cover two months for Madame O." Ora shifted and asked, "Zip me up?"

I did as she asked, wanting to do just the opposite with my zipper, yet knowing she wasn't going to let me go any further right then. I had gone from being a teasing prude with Raphael to a horned-up slut willing to screw anything that walked. Much of this false confidence was alcohol induced. I had planned to get wasted, and sex and drink had always been a winning couple, aiding and abetting many couplings.

She slipped into her high heels and added a short jacket made of pink boa feathers. "What do you think?"

"Gorgeous. You look super-hot."

"Thanks, doll. I'd kiss you but this face has to stay put until after the show. Sho taught us that. Once it's on, it doesn't come off until we're done. I miss her."

Together we started to walk out of the dressing area.

"Don't worry about Sho. I'm sure she's safe," I added to calm her down.

Ora relaxed and kept talking. "Polly heard from her."

"Recently?"

"Just yesterday."

Then she realized her mistake. It had been a slip and she knew it. No one was supposed to know, except the girls at 801.

"Promise me you won't say a thing, Nick. I have such a big mouth. I'd be in such trouble with everyone. Please, promise. Promise."

She was on the verge of tears. I wanted to hug her, but knew I'd be rebuffed because she didn't want her facial creation to be disturbed in any way.

"Don't worry. Just tell me she's okay."

Ora looked around to see if anyone was listening.

Dale, the soundman, was checking out the music. I could hear bits of Cher playing in the background as a few of Sho's protégés started to come upstairs for the nine o'clock show. Ora was afraid they might have overheard. But lyrics about loneliness, loss, and stardom overshadowed Ora's pleas. Before she got away, I caught her arm, hoping to get more information. She looked at me in alarm.

"You don't have to say another word. Just nod if she's okay."

Ora turned around again, realized she wouldn't be saying anything, then looked directly at me with a conspiratorial smile and gave me the briefest of nods as she walked out into the cabaret area.

"Miss Ora, you timed that perfectly. You didn't have to do any of the work hustling customers," Sin said.

"You can be such a bitch."

As they entered backstage to prepare for the show, I got ready to leave, knowing that Sho had been in touch with her girls and she was safe.

"Why don't you stay for the show?" Ora asked.

"Might come to the eleven, but I want to wander about and see if I can get into trouble."

"If you haven't found it, come back later, and I'll make sure you get some—trouble, that is," she said, and smiled.

I'm sure you would, I thought.

10

Getting drunk was easy, but I found it wasn't that much fun by myself. I should have asked Norm to come with me and let my mother sit on the porch. I laughed out loud at the visual and then remembered I should be quiet so I didn't wake them inside, since the windows would be open.

But when I entered the house, I heard strange sounds coming from down the hall. Someone must be awake.

"Norm, Norm, is that *shoe*?" I slur-shouted. "*Yhere*?" I tried again as I bumped into an end table. I wondered where my mother was.

I heard some muffled talking and shuffling coming from the bedroom. Then I saw him stumble out of his room while trying to pull up his shorts. I thought it a bit odd because he always slept in his boxers or so I thought.

"Nick. Ahh. I wasn't expecting you so soon." He was sweating and his eyes kept darting back toward his bedroom, and he had a boner.

"I heard something about Sho," I said, excited that I was able to share something new about the case.

67

"We need to talk," Norm said.

As I got closer, he pushed me away from his room toward the living room. Strange. As I got closer, I heard someone in his room clear her throat.

"Oh, I'm sorry. I didn't mean to interrupt."

"Nick, I shouldn't have crossed…" This piqued my curiosity.

As I pushed past him, I saw her, my mother, in Norm's bed. She was trying to hide by pulling the blanket up to her neck. At first, I thought I was hallucinating. What was she doing in Norm's bed? And then it all came together. I felt betrayed and wasn't sure why.

I looked at Norm, then at my mother, and instinctively pulled my arm back and hit him squarely on the jaw. He wasn't expecting it and reeled back. I had landed a good punch and he was bleeding. Under any other circumstances, he would have been proud of me. When I tried to do it again, he recovered enough to put his arms around me and hold me in a bear hug.

"Let me go, you son of a bitch. How could you?"

"Nicky, stop it. Stop it right now," my mother yelled from the bed.

"Why? You don't want me to hurt your lover? Is that it?"

She wrapped the blanket around herself and came out to the hallway.

"Stop fighting and sit down. I want to talk to you."

"What's there to talk about?"

"Stop acting like a child. We're all adults."

Norm realized I was over my initial shock and let me go.

"I'm out of here. I don't need to hear explanations."

"Show some respect. She's your mother."

"Respect? She doesn't deserve it. You two have probably been doing this a while. Boy, paint me stupid."

"Nicky. Sit down. Let's talk this out," Wanda pleaded.

"There's nothing to talk about. I'll be staying somewhere else so you two can have all the privacy you want." I went up to my room, threw a few things in my bag, and headed out of the house, but Norm blocked my way.

"Nick, you need to talk with your mother," he said, but he still had an erection, so it was difficult to take him seriously. He seemed aware of this and swallowed uncomfortably.

"And who do you think you are, my new father? I don't think so." I tried to push him aside. I was acting like a petulant child and knew it. I just couldn't help it. None of it made sense. They were single adults. They had both lost their spouses. If she wasn't my mother, and he wasn't my partner, I'd be happy for both of them. Yet, I felt they had cheated on me.

He told me my mother was coming to visit, but I didn't think she was coming to shack up with him. Then this small animal came running in and started barking. The only light in the house was coming from Norm's bedroom, and at first, I thought it was another Key West creature and backed away. This one barked and barked and seemed ready to attack.

"What's that?"

"That's my new dog, Nathan. I just got him last week. He's a rescue and so cute and loving. I thought I'd surprise you," my mother said.

"You surprised me. That's for sure. But believe me, you and Norm are a much bigger surprise than Nathan will ever be."

"Norm, do you think you can give us a moment. I'd like to talk to Nick alone."

"Sure. Sure. No problem," Norm said, and went to his room.

In the meantime, she had slipped on a terrycloth robe.

She picked up Nathan to quiet him down and tried to take my hand to lead me to the sofa in the living room. I pushed her hand away. I didn't want anything to do with her.

"I'm sorry that you found us this way. It definitely wasn't planned. In fact, none of this was planned, but I don't need to explain that to you."

"Then why are you trying to?" I asked, knowing I was blurring my words.

"Have you been drinking?" she asked.

"Have you been fucking?" I countered.

"Nick, that's enough," Norm yelled from the bedroom.

"I need to tell you something, Nicky," Wanda said.

Trying to understand the psychological boundaries of two significant people in my life, while my libido raged on like a Santa Ana–fueled brushfire, made me feel as helpless as Alice falling down the rabbit hole. Knowing *inebriated* had joined in the merriment didn't make my descent any easier.

Then I heard my mother's familiar voice trying to bring me back to her reality. "As you know, your father has been gone seven years. Since then, I haven't seen anyone, but I've felt if the right person came along, I'd be open to it. I had even thought of joining one of those dating sites."

"You didn't tell me."

"And that's my point, Nick. I don't have to."

"I know that." I felt myself softening. She was right.

"Have I ever told you who you should sleep with?" was her volley after my brilliant serve. She could never allow defeat and waited for the precise moment to lob the game ball back midair, hoping to catch me off guard.

I responded by not saying a word.

"Have I?" she asked, relentless.

"No," and she had scored. It was faultless and true.

"I didn't think that was my right, and I've always believed that. I worried like any mother and hoped you'd make the right choices. You found Darren and we accepted him."

The game was put on hold as the real issue came center stage.

"But, why Norm? Anyone else but—"

"Norm. He's your partner, not your lover. You don't want to share him with anyone. Doesn't he have choices?"

Apparently not. My bad.

"In a lot of ways, he's been a substitute for Darren. Caring and supportive."

"Stop right now," my mother said. "It's only right if *you* decide it's right, Nick. But I am also an adult woman with needs. Your father isn't around, and he didn't care much about sex."

"I don't want to hear it!" I yelled, covering my ears.

I felt like a teenager being forced to listen to a parent's sex life. It was beyond torture.

"Neither of us cheated on the other because we took our vows seriously."

"Mom, I don't—"

"I'm getting older, Nicky, and I'm going to grab pleasure where I can. Norm is kind and caring, and we slept with each other. Expressing love for another person is a good thing. Life is short."

I stumbled back a step and remained quiet as I considered what she said. Logically, it made sense, but I felt sick. It could have been the booze, but I didn't think so. It was too much to process in my state.

I got up. "Knock yourself over," I said, knowing my drunkenness had made that come out wrong, not remembering the correct saying.

I wanted to make a dramatic exit but stumbled into the wall instead, as I made my way to the front door. Norm came out to see what happened when he heard the thud.

"Nicky, come back."

Norm stopped her as she started to come after me.

"Let him go, Wanda. He'll figure it out."

11

I had no idea where I was going. I needed air. I needed to be out of that house, away from both of them. As I walked toward Duval Street, I realized I had forgotten my duffel bag. For all practical purposes, I was homeless. I had to laugh to myself. I had left a two-million-dollar resort to roam the streets.

I had already been to the 801 and wanted to avoid another love-fest with the girls. Instead, I walked into Bourbon Street Pub, the gay bar across the street from the 801. Locals just called it Bourbon Street. It drew in a different crowd, since there were foreign male strippers, most of them Russian, dancing on the bar. I looked at them and although they certainly caught my eye, I wasn't interested in ogling. I wanted to sit alone and think. I saw a group walking toward the back and followed them. I realized many of the waitstaff and workers had accents and wondered why there was such a large group of Slavic immigrants here in Key West.

"Hey, gorgeous you, have seat," someone yelled in a foreign accent. I tried to focus and realized it wasn't anyone I knew personally. I could have been in a bar in Mother Russia.

"Thanks." But I pointed toward the back.

As I exited the back door, I found a much smaller bar, which I later learned was called the Garden Bar. It was designed as a tiki hut and didn't hold more than twenty people. There was a pool within ten feet of it and some customers were lying on chaises, a few of them nude.

I found a seat at the far corner and settled in. The bartender, a gym rat baring his well-built chest, couldn't have been more than twenty-five. He wore bright diamond studs, giving his angular face an impish quality.

"How you doing tonight?" he asked in a Russian accent. *Another Russian,* I thought. *Well, Key West winters sure beat Moscow's.*

"I've had better," I answered.

"Hmm. What can I get you?"

"Vodka tonic," I said, doing my best to avoid slurring, not that it mattered much here.

He brought my drink and I paid him, leaving a healthy tip.

"Thanks, dude. You look familiar."

"I hear that a lot. A common face."

"I wouldn't say that. It's a great face."

"Thanks," I said, and then looked pointedly into my drink, hoping he'd get the hint I didn't feel like talking. He may have been young, but he was savvy. He immediately turned and went to the other end of the bar to wait on other customers.

I took a big swig and let out a relaxing sigh, happy to get away from the nightmare scene I had just experienced.

I wanted to sit and chill until I decided my next move, but my thoughts were interrupted by a familiar voice asking, "Hey, Nick. How's it going?"

Raphael sidled up to me. "What brings you here?"

I shrugged, focusing on following the train of thought.

"How about you?"

"It's one of my hangouts." Then he smiled and said, "It's a hot spot to pick up guys."

And that was the last thing I remembered.

12

NO HOLDS BARRED

I woke to the sound of someone knocking. I felt as if each knock was the town crier's bell bouncing off my skull. I got the warning and needed to stop it before the knells killed me. My mouth was dry, I was thirsty, and I felt miserable.

When I threw off the sheet, I saw I was buck-naked and didn't know where I was. At least there wasn't someone else next to me. I had another blackout last night. I looked for my clothes and saw my jeans neatly folded over a chair. I doubted I had the where-withal or coordination to accomplish such a task and wondered if I had been kidnapped by someone else with OCD. I slipped them on and opened the door.

Raphael was standing there, smiling, and holding a tray.

"Can I come in?"

"How do I know you haven't been in already?" I tried to smile but even that hurt. "I don't remember much of last night."

Ever since Darren's murder, I started to drink more and this wasn't my first blackout. I couldn't stop thinking I was somehow responsible for Darren's death. What frightened me the most was how vulnerable and helpless I made myself in these bouts. My thoughts made me wonder about the recent Key West victims and if they were in a helpless state so the killer could easily maneuver them without resistance.

"I can assure you, your virtue and everything else are intact," Raphael said, interrupting my train of thought.

Since I couldn't remember what happened, I decided to believe him. I didn't want to think about the alternatives.

"How did I get here? And where is here?"

"Take a seat. I'll explain all."

I grabbed my shirt and realized it smelled of stale cigarette smoke and day-old Stoli. I wrinkled my nose. I hesitated putting it on but didn't have a choice. I felt too naked without a shirt, even though Raphael must have undressed me to put me to bed.

"Do you have any—"

"Aspirin? Right here, and I brought you some juice and water to wash them down. You're dehydrated. Drink it all."

I noticed he had also brought a steaming pot of coffee. Each time I started to ask him a question, he shushed me. Somehow he recognized I was living the *walk of shame* and wanted me to get a handle on it. I appreciated his kindness and didn't have the energy to question his motives. He was taking care of me and that felt good. It reminded me of what Darren and I had, and I found I wasn't feeling as anxious around him as I had before.

After two cups, black, no sugar, thank you, the cobwebs cleared, but most memories of the previous night were gone, too.

He explained that he found me at the Garden Bar, that I hadn't been feeling any pain, and that I had spilled my guts out about

Norm and my mother. Then I accepted his sympathetic invitation to stay at his cousin's place, much like Blanche DuBois depending on the kindness of strangers.

For this I was grateful and let out a satisfied sigh. I felt safe around him and knew he wasn't a jerk just trying to get into my pants, although that thought wasn't as unpleasant this time around.

"I left a clean pair of my jeans and a T-shirt in the bathroom. They might be too big but you can leave your clothes outside the door, and I'll throw them in the washer. You're welcome to stay here until you decide what you want to do."

I knew what I wanted to do and it didn't involve wearing clothes.

"That sounds like a plan," I said, "but before I decide anything else I need a long hot shower."

He looked at me with those deep, dark bedroom eyes, and it took what little impulse control I had left not to fall into his arms right then. My only issue was that I hadn't brushed my teeth.

"There's also a robe in there if you prefer, but your clothes will probably be ready by the time you've showered and had more coffee. That way you'll have clean clothes when you leave."

I hadn't planned on a quick departure, but maybe he wasn't interested in me any longer. After all, I was the one who had acted squirrelly.

The water pressure was good and the pounding hot water and steam from the shower opened my sinuses and rinsed away the emotional grime from the night before. I still couldn't get my head wrapped around Norm and Wanda. It was one of the few things I remembered from last night and wished I hadn't. I could forgive my mother, but I felt betrayed by Norm, even though it didn't make any sense. In my tired and confused mind, he had crossed an unspoken boundary.

I tried on Raphael's clothes, but he had broad shoulders and the jeans were a size too big, so I wrapped the white terrycloth robe around myself instead. Normally, I was more open about nudity, but I was still somewhat embarrassed about my behavior with him. What excited me the most was finding a packaged toothbrush, toothpaste, and mouthwash, which allowed me to feel minty clean.

Finding that I was alone, I poured another cup of coffee and checked the messages on my phone, which I had found on the kitchen table. There was an old one from Jojo, who was a good friend and colleague back in Chicago. Norm and I had invited him to visit us in Key West.

> Am taking you up on your invite.
> Want to help with the case. Also
> want to see Merlot.

Merlot, I thought. *Who was that?* I wondered. I texted him back.

> C'mon down. Glad to have you
> here even if it's to see some wine
> When are you coming in?

I heard a knock on the door and smiled, knowing Raphael was behind it. I was wearing a clean robe. His robe. I also had fresh breath. Two things I was in control of. That was important.

Raphael gave me a big smile when he came in.

"Your clothes should be ready in about ten minutes." He gave me that seductive stare again.

"Thanks," I said.

"You look good in that robe," he said. "Keep it."

"I couldn't. It's yours."

"That's the point. I like the idea of being wrapped around you, even if it's by way of my robe."

He came a step closer and I felt my heart skip a beat.

"Of course, I know you'd look a lot better with it off."

Maybe it was his kindness, maybe I was still drunk, maybe I was just horny, but this time I wanted him closer. When he saw I didn't move away, he untied the knot holding the robe closed, slipped it off me, and pulled me toward him.

When he moved in to kiss me, I let him. His full lips were soft and hungry and I pushed back with mine. I felt my face flush as we each applied more pressure against the other. I reached for his shirt and pulled it over his head. Then I grabbed his shorts and unbuckled the belt. I wanted him. All of him.

"Would you like to or would you prefer—"

Raphael was being generous in letting me decide. I appreciated it. "Do you have a condom?" I asked, letting him know I would "bottom," feeling it was a way of thanking him.

Darren and I had changed positions during our time together. It all depended on our moods, but I wanted to keep Darren out of this. I wasn't going to let memories of him stop me this time. This was mine. Besides, Darren had left me, even though through a tragedy. That anger wasn't completely gone, but neither was the guilt.

Rather than analyzing every negative feeling, I allowed myself to embrace the good ones. I enjoyed Raphael's skin against mine. He was hairier than me. His shoulders were broader and his legs more muscular.

"You have a great body," I managed to say when our mouths weren't busy.

"Shut up so I can enjoy yours," he said playfully, as we returned to liplock.

It all seemed to flow naturally, like a well-choreographed ballet. Often the first time can be awkward and clumsy, but we didn't seem to have that problem. In fact, after an hour, we did it again to prove the point.

While still in bed, we jokingly spoke pillow/cop talk.

"You were an accessory to several lewd acts," he said.

"But I surrendered on command," I chuckled.

"Are you ready to confess?" he asked

"Yes, Officer."

"I'll Mirandize you."

"I thought you did."

"Not completely."

"If that's what it's called, please do it again."

"Always a pleasure to serve," he said.

I awarded him with a kiss and we both laughed.

Once I was dressed, I asked, "Anything new on the cases?"

"We're still waiting on the results from Miami. Things take longer down here and we have the holidays to contend with, too. But having family in the right places can speed things up," he added. "I have a cousin who works there. I'll call him."

"Speaking of, one of our team members, Dr. Jojo, sent me a text saying he's coming down, and he offered his expertise. Do you mind?"

"Procedurally it's not correct, but if you don't say anything, I won't, especially if it helps us solve the case."

"Great, and who's Merlot?"

"Why?"

"Dr. Jojo made a point of saying he plans on seeing Merlot."

"She's a novelty strip act. Twice a year she appears at the Red Garter. It's usually standing room only. Truly, one of those Only in Key West events."

13

I decided to go back to the house, despite my discomfort.
Maybe after getting laid, things would take on a new perspective. If
nothing else, I was much more relaxed. Note to self: Sex is the best
drug out there and doesn't require a script.

Raphael dropped me off on the way to HQ and said, "Call me
if you need me for anything." Then he gave me one of his devilish
smiles and said, "I promise I'll be *up* for it."

He chuckled, gave a toot of his horn, and was gone. I stared at
the bumper of his convertible with several ONE HUMAN FAMILY
stickers on it, and already wished we were back at the guesthouse.

I walked up to the door and wasn't sure whether I should knock
or not. I had a key, of course, but considering the turn of events, I
decided knocking was the wise thing to do. No reason to start the
day off badly. I was more hurt than angry and wasn't sure why.

Norm came to the door. He tried to smile but one side of his
mouth was swollen. I wondered how he got that and then I remembered I had slugged him.

Nice going, Nick, I thought, feeling like a complete ass.

83

"Nick, come in. Why are you knocking?" And then he sensed my discomfort about last night, and he looked down at his feet as he said, less boisterously, "We're having breakfast. Join us."

"*Nickala,* I've been so worried," Mom said as she ran toward me.

She hugged me but I didn't return the hug, and her eyes welled up with tears as she turned away. Usually, I would've received a lecture, but we were a long way from normal. It would take a while for the dust to settle, and for the first time, I saw my mother as a vulnerable woman who needed to be loved.

"Come join us for some coffee," she said. "I'm so glad you're all right."

Norm and my mother made love, I thought. *It had nothing to do with me.* I found myself softening to the idea. How different was that from my morning with Raphael?

I took a seat and my mother poured me some coffee.

"Norm, I don't know if I told you what I found out about Sho."

He paused and said, "I don't think you finished. I'd like to hear it, though."

So this was the new "normal." My mom was sleeping with Norm. I was sleeping with Raphael. We would all pretend there weren't any underlying hostilities.

Life moved on regardless of who was zooming whom. Maybe my mom was right: Life's too short to think otherwise.

14

"Let's go sit by the pool," Norm said.

"Great. I'll get a cup and join you," Wanda said.

Norm and I looked at each other, unsure of how to handle this. As much as my mother wanted to help, I knew I didn't want her involved in the case. This was police business and had nothing to do with her personally. I wasn't sure how Norm felt about it, but I couldn't imagine he'd want her involved, either. This was his call. The pause that lingered in the room hung there like a helium balloon, swaying back and forth. It would either disappear into the stratosphere or burst in front of us.

"I don't think that's a good idea, Wanda," Norm said.

My mother wasn't one to take no for an answer.

"Why not? I may be able to catch something you miss."

"This isn't a game of Clue. We were asked to be consultants by the chief of police. I don't mean to sound harsh, but the answer is no. This is official business, and I don't think he'd like to hear we were sharing confidential information with an outsider." After Norm finished, I could see him wince. He knew he shouldn't have ended his sentence with "outsider."

"Norm, last night, you didn't treat me like an *outsider*," she said, glaring at him.

"I'm taking Nathan for a walk in the backyard, while the two of you sort this out," I said, repressing a smile. Their first fight, and for once Norm would experience a *Wanda guilt trip*. I was still hung over as I went to make a drink, and thought, *I really do need to cut back*. I struggled with this for a while and finally decided to pour only one shot of bourbon rather than two into my coffee. Nathan scooted out ahead of me, and I closed the door behind us.

While the small dog nosed around, I sat by the pool, sipping the soothing liquid and feeling myself start to unwind. It was early and I enjoyed the warm sun as I lay back to relax. I took a deep breath of the ocean air. His investigations complete, Nathan decided to take a nap in my lap and was soon emitting snores. It felt so good not to be part of the kitchen drama. When I thought about it, I realized it truly was kitchen kitsch and laughed. Sometimes I really cracked myself up.

As much as I wanted to stay out of it, I couldn't help hearing their conversation.

"'Outsider' was the wrong word, Wanda. I'm sorry. I didn't mean that," Norm said.

"Good. Let's go outside and join Nick. I've always wanted to be a detective."

"You're missing the point, Wanda."

"No, *you* are. I'm not the kind of woman you can use and then shut out of your life."

"Don't take this personally, Wanda. This situation is very unique and certainly not one Nick or I expected."

"What? My sleeping with you or discussing the case?"

"Wanda, I like you. I had a great time last night. I thought you did, too. Now, I have to go do my job with Nick and with Nick alone. Why don't you enjoy the house? Go shopping? Take a tour? I'll be back later."

"Don't worry, Norm. I can find things to do. But I won't forget you've shut me out. There are a lot of other fish in the sea," she said. "Some are harmless. Others not. I was hoping you weren't a shark." After that, she turned and went to her room.

Norm joined me outside. His shoulders sagged and he avoided eye contact. "You want to take a ride and discuss the case?"

"Sure."

A moment passed. I knew what it was like to have an argument with someone you cared about. I bit my lip. This no longer had anything to do with my mother. This was about pain, hurt, and relationships. *Awkward* had pulled up a chaise and was considering staying a while. Norm and I got up and went to the car in silence, deciding to leave Awkward behind to enjoy the pool by himself.

"Where do you want to go?" I asked.

"Let's just drive around. We can talk while we drive. That's what we've always done, right?"

"Right."

15

We drove for a few minutes, and Awkward, although unin-vited, had tagged along. In fact, he even had the audacity to sit between us. I opened the window and let the fresh air wash over me, while Norm stared straight ahead. It was another beautiful day, except for the atmosphere. Neither of us had said a word since we got in the car. After five uncomfortable minutes, I blurted, "Perez and I slept together."

Norm chuckled. Then he snorted and finally he let out a loud, uproarious laugh. It was one of those laughs that was contagious. Soon, I joined him. We were both laughing so hard Norm had to pull over to the side of the road and park. Each time one of us stopped, the other would start. This lasted ten minutes, until we couldn't laugh anymore. My sides ached.

"Must be in the air," I said.

"Or the water," he said.

"Aren't we the pair?" I asked.

"Are you staying with him?" Norm asked as he resumed driving.

"No. His cousin has a private guesthouse a few blocks away. It's convenient and the only way I can seem to be able to handle it. Close but not too close, if you know what I mean. It's only temporary."

"Does he have another cousin with a guesthouse?" Norm asked.

After this morning, I knew exactly what he meant.

"By the way, Norm, I'm sorry I went off on you last night."

"No apologies necessary, bud. It certainly wasn't planned."

"Plus, I was loaded."

"I get it."

"I think the part that made me the angriest was that you continued to have a boner the whole time you were trying to apologize and—"

"About that. I had taken two Viagra and it was beyond my control, Nick. It had been a long time and—"

"Oh. Oh. I see," I said, suppressing a smile.

Like a champagne bottle being opened, our feelings exploded at each other. Had it been any other situation, we would have continued with the party. But it was too much too soon, and a silence stopped the celebration as quickly as it had begun.

This was as far as we were willing to go in sharing our intimacies, and I couldn't help but think it was natural fallout after last night's confrontation. I longed to have our comfortable relationship back. I knew it would return, but it would take time.

The uncomfortable silence lingered. We were both searching for a way to communicate. Then, we fell back into partner routine, which was completely safe territory.

"I stopped in at 801 last night and—" I started.

"You were going to tell me about Sho," Norm said.

We were at a point where we often knew what the other was thinking and regularly completed each other's sentences. We had become intimate professionals.

"Yeah, I was chatting up Ora, who was in a very talkative mood, and she slipped and said they had heard from Sho."

"Is she okay?"

"Yes, but that's all Ora would say. She became really paranoid after that and wouldn't say another word. But you were right. The girls knew more than they were letting on."

"Have you told Perez?" Norm asked.

"Not yet."

"What about Mimi and the scratches?"

"I don't think they're from camping."

"Me neither."

"Perez say anything else about that?"

"We were distracted." I gave a lewd grin.

"No details, please," Norm said.

"Don't worry. I didn't plan on giving you any."

I wasn't even sure what was going to happen between us, but when I thought about Raphael, a warm glow kindled inside me. I wanted to see him again, but at the same time I felt like I was cheating on Darrell. It was difficult to erase fifteen years of history.

"We need to talk to Mimi," Norm said.

"I agree, but where can we find her?"

"Maybe one of the girls can help," I said.

It was only 11:00 a.m. and it was doubtful any of them would be at the cabaret. I wondered if 801 was even open. We had driven around the island and were approaching Duval Street. Few people walked the streets before noon, making it look like a ghost town.

"I forgot to tell you. I got a text from Jojo."

"And?"

"He's coming down to visit."

"Great!"

"He wants to help with the case."

"But that isn't procedure."

"I know people."

Norm laughed. "Sleeping your way to the top, are you?"

"If you weren't driving, you'd get a jab," I said. "Jojo has another reason, too."

"I'm listening."

"He's coming down to see Merlot," I said.

"He's coming down to see some wine?"

"She's a specialty stripper appearing at the Red Garter Saloon on Duval Street this week."

Norm laughed again, and we were off. If anyone saw us they would probably think we were high, and we were. Our endorphins had come out to play, running free, frolicking in the field of our minds. Then my cell phone rang.

16

It was Raphael.

"Just thinking about you. I had a great time this morning."

"Me too," I said, smiling, and I turned to face the window, as if that would shield me from exposing my feelings in front of Norm. "Any developments on Sho or the suicides?" I asked.

"You can't talk."

"Right."

"That means I can talk dirty to you and you'd have to listen."

"Any other time, I'd encourage you," I said.

"I'm getting hard just thinking about you," he said, ignoring my situation. "When can I see you again?"

"Soon."

Raphael was being naughty and enjoying every minute of it. If Norm weren't there I probably would have joined in. Raphael certainly knew how to push my buttons and that scared me. We hardly knew each other.

I started to feel more uncomfortable and changed the subject. "Do you know how we could reach Mimi?"

"I have a few ideas."

"Also, who worked the suicides?"

"Detectives Warren and Bridges, I believe. Let me make a few calls and I'll get back to you."

I looked over at Norm, even though I knew I was blushing, and saw he was smiling, looking a little nervous. As professional partners, we'd have to work hard to avoid sharing too much information about our intimate partners.

Five minutes later the phone rang again.

"Mimi will meet you at the New York Pasta Garden restaurant in Duval Square, Virginia and Simonton. She'll be there in fifteen. Detectives Warren and Bridges did work the other suicides if you want to follow up. I alerted them you might want to talk to them."

"Thanks. Later."

The Italian restaurant was literally in the center of Duval Square, a shopping mall in the middle of town, filled with small businesses: Island Radio; Grateful Guitar; Headline, a beauty salon; and a few real estate companies.

Although it had all the quaint trappings of a European town square, the place looked like an anomaly compared to the rest of Key West. Maybe it was the asphalt parking lot that served as the back entrance or all the concrete that surrounded the businesses, but I didn't get any sense of quirkiness. It could have been any strip mall filled with assorted stores.

The New York Pasta Garden had made an effort to distinguish itself from the other businesses. It had open-air tables, Italian water fountains, and banyan trees that housed screeching but colorful macaws. Occasionally, the owner would put one of the macaws on his shoulder and walk around, asking the customers how they were enjoying their meal. One of the macaws might answer, "Yum, yum." If it didn't, the maître d' would carry on a conversation with the bird.

When the maître d' saw us looking around, he approached and asked, "Table for two, gentlemen?"

"We're here to meet someone," I said.

"Can I help? It's a small town."

"Mimi? Mimi Peters?"

He used his menu to point in the direction of where Mimi was sitting at a table on the edge of the square. She was dressed in a tight-fitting white V-neck and gray shorts, and talking on her phone.

We joined her and the first thing we noticed were the scratches on her arms. Norm and I gave each other a look that confirmed what we thought. She had definitely tried to cover them with makeup and was continuing to do so, but there were too many and they were too deep to conceal.

"Hey, Mimi, good to see you," I said.

"Thanks for meeting us," Norm added. "Really enjoyed your song, 'Bottoms Up,' the other night."

"What can I do for you?" she asked coldly, avoiding all pleasantries.

She was on the defensive, reminding me of a turtle protected by a hard shell, only showing its head if necessary.

"We're here about Sho."

"Have you found her?"

"Not yet. We wondered if you knew anything about her."

"No, why would I?"

"Just asking. It's routine. I saw you get in the ambulance with her," I said.

She wasn't only being defensive; she was being downright hostile, making me wonder what she was hiding.

"You and the EMTs were the last ones to see her."

"I was just checking on her. They let me out as soon as I saw that she was okay. The EMTs will vouch for me—what's this about, anyway? Am I under suspicion?"

"Should you be?" I asked.

"Not unless you're out to get drag queens," she said defiantly, trying to make this into a personal attack.

"How'd you get those deep scratches, Mimi?" Norm asked, ignoring her remark.

Mimi acted like she was being singled out. Her fear seemed different from that of the other girls, who were afraid for Sho and Matt.

"Not that it's any of your business, but I went camping over the weekend."

"Where do you camp?"

"Wherever I can," she said, and gave a fake laugh at her joke. "You guys should try it sometime. Everyone knows you're a gay couple."

We had heard this before and ignored it. People often attack when they feel trapped. Mimi was feeling cornered about something. *What*, was the question.

"Anyone camp with you?" I asked.

"No. I like to go by myself. It relaxes me."

"Where's Sho?" Norm asked.

There was a pause. Mimi looked at both of us defiantly, straightened her back, stood up, and said, "If you have any more questions, contact my lawyer. She's right down Southard. Her name's Trudi Lewis. I'm sure she'd be glad to talk to you. Bottoms up, guys." She turned and left in a huff, knowing we were watching her.

Nothing like a queen's dramatic exit, I thought.

"What do you think?" I asked Norm.

"I think she's lying. She knows more about Sho and we need to find out what."

"We should talk to the 801 girls again."

17

It was 1:00 p.m. and the customers nursing their drinks at the 801 were quiet, recovering from the night before.

Billy, the bartender, greeted us. "Hey, officers. What can I get you?"

"Coke for me," I said.

"Make that two," Norm added.

We made ourselves comfortable in the row of seats facing outside. The shutters were open, so you could not only see the customers inside, but also watch the colorful characters on the street.

Hearing familiar voices arguing, I turned my head toward the stairs and asked, "What's going on?"

"They're supposed to be having a rehearsal but it sounds like a free-for-all. Sho's not here to control it."

"Mind if we check it out? We have a few questions."

"Knock yourselves out."

A velvet rope, not more than two feet high, blocked the entrance to the steps and I navigated it quickly, but Norm was staring like it was an eight-foot hurdle. After some heavy breathing and slow maneuvering, he managed to get to the steps, but I couldn't let it go.

"And Malone clears it. The crowd screams in triumph," I teased.

Norm shot me a killer look, puckered his lips, and slammed his right fist into his left palm. I was glad I had already started up the steps. I would have certainly received a cuff.

The girls were in their street clothes, not wearing makeup or costumes. Some sat at the bar, others were perched on the stage. They looked like any group of people meeting together, but we soon found out that we had walked into a catfight.

"I've always been Sho's backup," Polly said.

"You were probably blowing her," Ora said.

"I'm the only one here who knows fashion and design," Sin said. "And I can sew the costumes."

"The only needles you use aren't for sewing. I should do costumes," Shaneeda Lay argued.

"You were hustling before Sho took you in. You're no Coco Chanel," Sin retorted.

"By the way, who took my pink wig? It was probably you, Canola. You like to squirrel away people's things and then claim them as yours," Ora said.

"You bitch. What would I want with that skanky thing? Have you looked in the restroom? That's where you spend most of your time with your groupies."

"At least I have some."

"Stop it. We need to rehearse," Polly yelled, failing to get any response.

Norm put his two fingers in his mouth and let out a loud whistle that got their attention.

"That's enough, ladies. From what I heard, Sho's coming back soon."

Norm's whistle stopped their bickering, but his announcement gave them a look of wonder and concern. Ora gave me a dirty look, knowing where Norm got the info. What did she expect? Norm was my partner and partners worked together. A cop's promise was like a drag queen's tits, a necessary illusion.

"How do you know that?" Shaneeda asked.

"I heard it from a reliable source."

"She can't come back," Zip Tease said.

"She'd put her life at risk," Sin added.

I smiled. Norm's experience showed. He knew nothing of the sort but he used the moment to elicit new information. Now we had heard from a second source that Sho was alive and in danger.

The question was, why? The only thing I could think of was that Moss may have put a hit on her. And now that he was dead, there was no way of stopping it. Usually, any order would have to come from him, and sometimes even that couldn't stop it once the process was in motion.

But Polly was savvy enough to stop any other leaks and quickly changed the subject. "This is our usual staff meeting." Adding some attitude, she said, "We usually don't expect outside guests like the police, but we try to cooperate.

"By the way, how'd you like the show the other night, guys?"

"Which one?" I asked.

"Touché," Polly said.

"That's a good name. Maybe I'll change mine from Shaneeda Lay to Tou Ché. What do you think, girls?"

"I think you should keep your mouth shut," Ora said, her words directed at Shaneeda. But Ora made eye contact with the group, telegraphing her message.

The tone in the room dropped to chilly with a chance of frost.

"I know Sho has been in touch with you," I said. "For her sake and Matt's, we need to know what she said and where she is. We're with you as far as keeping her safe."

"You say that, but we're a family. We protect and take care of each other no matter what," Polly said.

"What about Chief Perez? He's concerned," I said, feeling like his defender.

"You think because he's gay, he's going to take a special interest in us?" Ora asked.

"Yes, I do."

"He's also the chief of police," Ora said. "That's his first concern. He'd throw anyone under the bus, gay or straight, if it made him look good. That's what he's about."

"His only concern," Polly added.

"He's the Bubbas' puppet. They control this town. They have a network that goes way beyond any type of law and order. He wouldn't be where he is today if his papa wasn't so powerful," Sin said.

I took this all in, trying to decide how much of it was true. What mattered was how they perceived the chief's role. Bottom line, they didn't trust him. After hearing some of their comments, I couldn't help but wonder how much Raphael was invested in solving the case.

"I don't know him like all of you do, but he's concerned about Sho and Matt," Norm assured them.

There were scoffs and mumbles of discontent. The truth was, they knew him better than we did.

I didn't think we changed anyone's mind, and the troupe was starting to fall apart. Sho was the glue that kept this crew together, and she wasn't here to control these performers and soothe their ruffled feathers. As much as they loved Sho, many of them wanted to be stars. If I announced an immediate audition, they might kill for the opportunity; maybe one of them already had.

Realizing how much they wanted that, I announced, "I'm going to throw out a deal. If you help us find Sho, I'll have a special TV show for the 801 girls. Sho will be the main guest, but I'll make sure each of you gets a chance to showcase your act."

Norm glanced at me from the corner of his eye, and I knew I was walking a very dangerous and thin line. Mixing police work with show business wasn't kosher, and if Chicago's Lieutenant Brodsky found out about it, I could be in hot water, again. I felt this was worth the risk, though, and something they understood. The question was, *How much did they trust me?*

A silence like Sunday morning blanketed the room. Each girl was examining her dream. They all saw their name in lights with their own TV show. Some saw me as a conduit to that goal, while others wondered if it was just another bribe.

Polly was smart. She knew what I was doing. She was older. Her professional clock was ticking. Soon, her time would be up, but she was making sure there wouldn't be any more leaks.

"Thank you for that generous offer, Nick. We'll talk it over and get back to you. Right now we need to rehearse. If we don't get these new numbers down, Sho will be disappointed in us. If we don't look professional, we won't look good on your show, will we? So if you don't mind, we need to get back to work."

With that, she turned her back on us, stood in front of the girls, and said, "Okay, ladies, from the top. Sin, do the count."

"One, two, three." The girls snapped into performance mode and got back to their rehearsal, crossing their arms in unison, forming three rows and taking a step back, and then turning as a group.

We had been dismissed. Norm and I looked at each other and nodded. We made our way for the stairs.

"One, two, three, and out," I said.

"Ten-four," he said.

18

As we walked out, my phone dinged, indicating a text. Before I could pull it out of my pocket, three more quickly followed.

One was from Jojo.

> I've just landed. What's the plan?

> Grab a cab to Hidden Sands Resort. We'll meet you there.

> Coolio.

The next one was from Raphael.

> I want to see you tonight.

> Jojo just got into town.

> Do a meet, greet, and split.

> I'll see.

> Pizza? Movie? Kisses?

> Kisses for sure.

The third was from my mother.

> Is Norm with you?

I threw my head back and let out a sigh. The last thing I wanted to do was be the go-between for my mother and Norm. He saw me bite the corner of my lip, a sure sign I was pissed, as I sent her a text.

> I'm not going to do this, Mom.

> Yes or no? You can do that much.

> We're working.

> Thank you.

I shook my head.

"Any of that good news?" Norm asked.

"Jojo just landed. Raphael wants to get together, and my mother—"

"I get it."

I respected him for that. He knew the position I was in, and he didn't want to make it any worse than it was. He was a mensch.

We decided to go back to the house. We were both glad Dr. Jojo would be working with us. He was someone we knew and trusted beyond reproach.

We pulled up just as Jojo was paying his fare. The cabbie got out, opened the trunk, and handed Jojo his bag.

Jojo, a dwarf at four foot eight, was wearing flip-flops, a Green Parrot T-shirt, and ordinary gray shorts. He already looked more like a local than either of us. He must have changed at the Key West airport, because I had checked the weather report and it was twelve degrees in Chicago and snowing.

"Great to see you," I said as I ran over, bent down, and hugged him.

"Likewise," Jojo said.

"Hey, bud," Norm said, grabbing his hand.

"Hey, Norm. Gotta love this weather."

"Wait till you see the digs."

We went into the house. Norm took his bag and I led the way. I decided he could share my room. There were two queen beds.

When Jojo got a look at the place, he let out a long whistle.

"Now, this is better than the Ritz."

On cue, my mother walked out in an outfit she must have found at one of the small boutiques on Duval. She was wearing a low-cut white blouse, a deep-coral pair of shorts, and silver sandals that accentuated her long legs. She had had a mani-pedi and looked like she had lived here her whole life. I wouldn't have been surprised if she had been spray-tanned at a salon.

"I know we've met before. I'm Wanda, Nick's mom."

"Wow," Jojo said. "It's a pleasure to meet again, Ms. Scott."

"Wanda, please."

"Okay. Wanda, puleeze," Jojo emphasized the last word, implying his sexual longing for her. She let out a very sensual and inviting laugh. I wondered if this was the same mother who bore me.

"Hi, Norm," Wanda said, and went over and kissed him on the cheek.

"Hi-i-i," Norm stuttered.

Nathan ran in and tried to jump on Jojo, waiting to be picked up so he could kiss him.

"Who's this?" Jojo asked.

"Wanda brought Nathan with her. He's a rescue. Looks like he's taken a shine to you, Jojo."

Jojo bent down and scooped him up. As expected, Nathan lavished him with kisses. It was an instant bond. Nathan wouldn't stop and Jojo was enjoying every minute of it.

"Yes, yes. I love you, too," Jojo assured Nathan and gently put him down.

"Come here, Nathan," Wanda ordered. Nathan ignored her and kept running around Jojo.

"Nathan, come here," Norm tried in his command voice, but Nathan ignored him, too. His obedience training matched the level of his being housebroken. Both required work.

"Jojo, you'll be sharing my room. I'm not here most of the time," I said, not wanting to go into detail. "There are also a couple of air mattresses in the closet and a sofa bed downstairs," I said, wanting to get away from this circus. Norm gave me a "don't-leave-me-here-alone" look. I felt for him, but he had made his bed and Wanda was luxuriating in it. I headed up the stairs to show Jojo his room.

Nathan ran ahead of me. He had turned it into a game, and he definitely wanted to stay with Jojo.

I couldn't help but think that the house I once thought of as posh boutique lodgings for Norm and me was quickly turning into a shared hippie commune, certainly upscale but a collective community nonetheless.

I appreciated Jojo's silence as I led him upstairs. I wasn't feeling as angry at Norm or my mother, but I wasn't completely comfortable, either. I wanted to get back to my guest cottage as soon as possible. I was sure Jojo would be fine. I had never seen him flustered about anything. Besides, he had made his intentions clear from the start. He was here to see Merlot, and it sounded like he already had a crush on her.

"Here's your room. It's self-sufficient and you can come and go as you please." I gave him one of my duplicate keys. I'll introduce you to Raphael—I mean Chief Perez—later."

I noticed Jojo's eyebrows arch the tiniest of millimeters, or so I thought. In fact, I wondered if I had imagined it. Was I getting paranoid about sleeping with the chief? It certainly would raise more than an eyebrow back in Chicago. Here, I wasn't so sure.

Jojo whistled approvingly, indicating his surprise at his sumptuous room with a view. He walked to the sliding glass door that led to his own balcony. It overlooked the pool and the Atlantic Ocean. He pushed open the door and walked onto the balcony. You could hear the blue-green surf hitting the rocks and see the numerous sandbars that lay beneath the surface of the ocean. A group of gorgeous women tanning themselves on an adjacent beach saw Jojo and waved. He waved back.

"This really is incredible."

"I keep pinching myself every time I look out the window. Amazing how some people live like this—right?"

"Right. I can see why a lot of people want to come here for the winter."

We could have spent another fifteen minutes talking about the weather and the house, but I thought I'd cut to the chase.

"You mentioned you're a fan of Merlot. When are you going to see her?"

"She opens tonight at the Red Garter. I'll be at the first show—nine p.m."

"Have you met before?"

"No. I've only heard about her in our community. She's a real fox."

"I'll take your word for it."

With all our ulterior interests, our investigation was quickly becoming a soap opera nonpareil. All the twists and turns would delight the most demanding viewer.

"Come see her. I reserved three tickets for you, Norm, and me, but I'm sure I can get a couple more. I want all of you to join me."

The thought of a stripper named Merlot had certainly caught my attention.

19

After Jojo settled in, I decided to return to my refuge, Raphael's guesthouse.

When I left, Norm and Wanda were in the pool, holding each other close, so I assumed all was well between them. They reminded me of a couple of teenagers experiencing love for the first time, not wanting to let go of each other and sharing intimacies.

I originally planned to leave a note in case they were in their own room, but now I could tell them in person. I was still a bit uncomfortable being around them when they were involved, but it was getting easier. I remembered my mother's words: *Life is short* and the implied: *It's my turn, now.*

"Jojo's going to relax for a while. He's invited us all to see Merlot perform tonight at the Red Garter. I'm considering going. I'll ask Raphael if he wants to join us. You in?"

They had already finished a couple of Bloody Marys and were very relaxed.

"What does she do?" Mom asked.

"She's a stripper."

"How fun. Let's go, Norm. I've never been to a strip club."

"Sure. Why not? We're on vacation."

"I'll text you. I'm going to Raphael's place."

"*Nickala*, don't be like that. Stay with us."

"Maybe tomorrow. I'd like my own space right now," I said. "You must understand that."

There was a slight pause. "Whatever you like," Mom said, not applying any pressure or guilt. This was certainly a pleasant change. If this was one of the effects of being with Norm, I could learn to accept their relationship much more. Norm seemed to be able to handle her by being firm and not accepting her guilt trips, a feat unto itself.

"I'll text you. *Ciao.*"

On my way to the guesthouse, I wondered about their future. Could either of them sustain a meaningful relationship? Forget meaningful—could they sustain a relationship? No one knew the answer.

Both of them had been without partners for a while, and they seemed to enjoy each other. Each of them decided to be vulnerable and take the risk of caring for and possibly being hurt by the other. I thought they were well matched.

I'm not sure Norm and Wanda would have taken this step in Chicago. I wouldn't have laid money on it, but I doubted it.

Yet everyone was on vacation. I felt I was in a time warp of permanent contentment unlike anything any one of us had experienced. One we never wanted to leave.

My mom was capricious, often stubborn, but Norm didn't take any crap from her. Could they support each other in times of crisis? They had survived their first fight. That was important. One thing I could say for sure was I hadn't seen either of them so relaxed, ever. Raphael and I were also taking risks. All of us were in the honeymoon phase. Like teenagers in love, we were playing outside during a hurricane, not caring about the consequences.

I vowed not to get in the middle of this. In no way did I want their relationship affected by their connection to me.

20

I should have sent Raphael a text that I was coming over,
but he said he wanted to see me. As I approached I was taken aback
to see his convertible parked in front. I was even more surprised
to see a good-looking guy leave the cottage. Norm and I had dis-
cussed some of the questions that still required answers, and it was
time to ask the chief what he knew. But I had a more immediate
question for him.

"Who was that guy?"

There was a slight pause. "My cousin, Javier."

He either had a big family or was a great liar.

Raphael was sitting on the couch, drinking a beer, clad only in
loose sport shorts. He had slouched down so that his perfect chest
was screaming "Touch me," while his loose shorts said, "Slide me
off." I decided he had a lot of cousins. To deal with the other possibility was too painful right now.

As appealing as he appeared, I wanted something other than
sex. But immediately after that thought, I felt myself starting to get
hard and I couldn't keep my eyes off him.

"Raphael, we need to talk about the case."

"Come here and sit down," he said, flashing a sweetly seductive smile. I wanted him too, but I also wanted some answers. I was already fighting my hard-on. *Stick to the case. Stick to the case,* I told myself, hoping the repetition would work as it did when I learned my multiplication tables.

"Did your detectives check the roads beyond the ER? Any tire tracks down the side roads?"

"Why?"

"To see if the EMTs turned down one of them? It might be a clue to Sho's disappearance."

"None of them would do that."

So much for that question. It hadn't been done and it was shoddy police work.

"We questioned Mimi today."

Raphael barely nodded, not showing any interest.

I wondered why he tried to derail anything about the investigation I brought up. Should I spoil the moment or let it go?

"Sho's got deep scratches all over her arms. What if Sho's DNA had been there?"

He paused and said, "Don't overthink this. She goes camping all the time and that's how she comes back. Maybe she's into bears." Raphael smiled.

"Don't you think you should question her?"

"Naw, I know her. She's okay. Come closer."

He grabbed me with more force than I expected, and he pulled me down next to him. He looked deep into my eyes and then he kissed me. It was the most tender, soft, passionate kiss I had had in a long time, or at least since yesterday.

"I have to ask: Do you want us to help you solve these cases?"

"Can we talk about this later?"

I searched his eyes and realized as much as I wanted to know, I wanted him more.

Raphael's kiss lingered and was so sensuous I felt him making love to my soul.

My lips synched with his as our intensity built. We let our feelings flow fluidly from the tips of our toes up to our mouths and out our pores. He pulled me closer to him.

I took myself away from his mouth and began to kiss his ears, his eyes, and his neck. I could feel his skin and enjoyed his smell, a combination of salty ocean and sweaty musk.

Just as Raphael reached for my shorts, I heard my phone ding.

"Don't," he begged.

"I have to. It could be serious."

But his look made me decide serious would have to wait.

21

It was a text from Jojo.

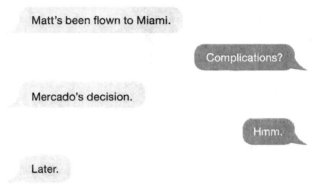

> Matt's been flown to Miami.

> Complications?

> Mercado's decision.

> Hmm.

> Later.

I called Norm to tell him the news, not knowing whether Jojo had let him know or given him any more specifics. It was unusual for Jojo not to discuss details, but I knew he preferred to do it in person.

Norm and I decided to meet for coffee at Denny's on Truman and Duval. We knew we could get a booth with some privacy. You could always count on Denny's.

"When?" Norm asked.

"Give me an hour. I have something to finish up," I said.

Raphael was my kryptonite. Although I wasn't impressed by his police work, I certainly found his body to be everything I'd hoped for and more.

Raphael said he had to get to his office. I noticed he named his own hours or used a concocted reason to return to HQ. He didn't seem to show much interest in the case and I was beginning to wonder why. Maybe the 801 girls were right about him.

Norm was already at the restaurant by the time I got there, and he didn't see me approaching. He was staring into his coffee, preoccupied. His brow was furrowed and he was holding on to the cup with his big mitts. If he could conjure up answers from staring, they would be popping up all over the table.

"What's up?"

He looked up at me and I could see that he may have been close to tears.

"You look like you need a hug."

Before he could get up, I leaned in and gave him one, even though I knew he didn't like them. If nothing else, it would shake him up a bit. He allowed me ten seconds before breaking free.

"I told you no," he said, annoyed.

I had a feeling my mom wanted to know more about the case and it was becoming an issue. "See, you're better already."

I had met up with Jojo earlier for a short briefing because he was my only other source I could trust.

"Jojo did some digging at the hospital and found out about Matt's transfer."

"Is he worse?" Norm asked.

"No, he's better, according to Jojo's sources, but that's what's strange about this. Mercado had him flown to Miami—usually done when a patient needs urgent care."

"We need to get to the bottom of this," Norm said.

"I think Mercado's protecting Sho and Matt," I answered.

"From what?" I questioned.

"If Sho's accident was caused by the commissioner, there'd be no reason for Matt to be moved, right?" Norm asked.

"But if the commissioner was a setup so everyone would think it's him, who is after Matt and Sho? I think we should talk to Mercado ourselves."

Norm nodded. "Get anything from Perez?"

I blushed the color of one of the red napkins that was on the table and didn't know why. It wasn't about the sex. I enjoyed that. I needed to work on my guilt. Raphael and I weren't doing anything wrong. I felt I was betraying Darren and that Norm disapproved. Nothing was further from the truth. He never even came close to insinuating anything, so I knew it was time for me to get a handle on this. If I continued to see Raphael, we'd be having a lot more sex. This was an issue to bring up with my therapist, and I dismissed that thought faster than it appeared. I was on vacation.

Norm laughed. "Let me rephrase. Did Perez offer any information to you that might be helpful?"

"That's just it. He doesn't seem to even want to talk about the case. He's treating it like a parking violation."

"I'm glad Jojo's here. He knows how we work. He can also follow up on the 801 girls' whereabouts after the accident. That would help."

I was looking at the menu and considering the new special—chocolate-chip pancakes, whipped cream, and sprinkles with hot links on the side—thinking I'd have to try it sometime.

"I'm having second thoughts about going to see Merlot. I'm not sure how I'll feel with my mom being with us," I said.

"No way, bud. Wanda and I are already committed. If you want, ask Perez. If nothing else, I guarantee you it will be one of those 'only in Key West' events."

We both laughed. I was beginning to get over my discomfort with Norm, and it was nice to be able to joke around again. We'd been through so much together.

22

Raphael had agreed to join us to see Merlot but I thought
I'd confirm.

"You still up for seeing Merlot tonight?"

"Sure. I've seen it before. It's fun. What time?"

"Show starts at nine p.m. Warning you—my mom is coming."

"I haven't bought the ring yet in case you were thinking of an
announcement." He laughed.

"You have a lot of time for that. If you pass her test, you can
pass anything."

"No worries. I'd like to meet her. I'll pick you up at eight thirty."

"Perfect."

Raphael and I had chemistry, but I never knew how serious he
was about anything other than sex.

Merlot was opening at the Red Garter Saloon on Duval Street,
sandwiched between a restaurant and a T-shirt shop. With all the
glam and glitz on Duval, somehow the club managed to look like an
after-hours joint from the 1920s.

We had all decided to meet in front of the club, but Jojo insisted
on going ahead of us so he'd make sure to get the right table, even

though he had reserved it. I had never seen him so concerned, since he always had a balanced attitude about everything.

I searched reviews on Yelp before going and found that the Red Garter was friendly to female customers. Many women said they enjoyed the show. I still felt uneasy going to a strip show with my mother, though, and repeated the same line Norm had said to me about going to 801's drag show, "'That if I feel uncomfortable, we leave.'"

"Fine with me, bud. I may be right behind you. Remember, we're going because Jojo was so insistent."

"You're right. Deal?"

"Deal."

Raphael and I were meeting Wanda and Norm in front of the club at eight forty-five.

Wanda wore black slacks, a pastel turquoise blouse, and diamond-studded earrings, making her look like she had come in from South Beach for the weekend, while Raphael sported tight black jeans and a Salt Life sport shirt, emphasizing his physique.

Norm and I wore shorts and V-neck shirts. I still hadn't figured out dress codes, but since the entertainment wouldn't be wearing anything, what we wore wasn't that important. No one would be looking at us.

After general introductions, Raphael said, "How nice to meet you, Mrs. Scott. Nick speaks so highly of you. I would have guessed you to be his sister rather than his mother."

"Thank you, Raphael. You don't mind if I call you Raphael, do you?"

"Not at all."

"Key West is lucky to have such a handsome chief of their police force."

So much for worrying about my mother and Raphael getting along. He had passed every test in record time. I glanced at Norm and he rolled his eyes.

After we entered the club, it took a minute to adjust to the darkness. The club made no attempt to be subtle. The lighting was whorehouse red: overhead recessed lights, strategically placed hurricane candles, Christmas LEDs underneath the bar. Medieval-style chandeliers with flickering-flame bulbs lit the middle room beyond the bar. Two enterprising decorators who owned a few clubs on the strip had achieved *Game of Thrones* chic.

Jojo waved to us as we entered and we went to meet him at a table directly in front of the stage. Norm and I exchanged an experienced glance, knowing the dangers of having a ringside seat after being at 801. I quickly introduced him to Raphael, who said how happy he was to have Jojo join us on the investigation.

Merlot was the featured performer and we knew we would have to sit through a few other acts before she came on. They were typical, if there was anything typical about opening acts at a strip club. I wondered if strippers ever smiled.

As I looked around the room, I saw that the audience was indeed mixed. There were several straight couples enjoying the show. The strippers didn't discriminate when it came to flashing their boobs from the stage. They were discerning, though, and instinctively knew which couples would allow them to flaunt their breasts in their faces or sit in a husband's lap.

I glanced over at my mother and found she was enjoying the show. Aside from liking Norm, I could tell she relished having a partner in her life again.

Norm was perspiring and had ordered two doubles in less than an hour. I had a sense he and I were the only prudes in the place when it came to this. We were old school.

Darren and I had vacationed at gay resorts a few times where clothing was optional, and I often went nude in that milieu, but this was a completely different scenario. I was sandwiched between my lover on one side and my mother on the other while watching female strippers—I struggled to keep myself calm.

Raphael was a Conch, meaning he had lived here his whole life and there wasn't much that fazed him about Key West. At Fantasy Fest, one of the biggest events in Key West, many women wore only their tattoos and body paint. Strangely enough, the city was attempting to crack down on this.

Jojo was there to see Merlot. Nothing and no one else mattered. She was up next.

The stage went dark, music was cued to the classic show song "Let Me Entertain You," the spot went on, and Merlot appeared.

"Welcome, ladies and gents. I'm Merlot and I'm here to entertain you."

She was dressed in a bright pink tutu, red bra, black top hat, and matching tails and wore six-inch red-sequined stilettos. She held a white poodle in her left arm. Halfway through her act, she kicked off her shoes, indicating a down-to-earth attitude.

"This is my dog, Gigi, and she's a bigger ham than I am. Isn't that right, Gigi?"

On cue, Gigi barked and licked Merlot's cheek. Merlot marched back and forth across the stage with a presence that indicated she owned it. I guessed her to be in her mid-forties.

Norm leaned over and said, "She looks like one of those pudgy angels by that famous painter Rubens."

We nodded in agreement. Norm's description was perfect, except I had a feeling Merlot wasn't an angel. She had a mischievous look in her eye that made everyone at our table smile. Jojo was gawking.

"Watch it. You never know what's going to fall into that mouth around here."

Merlot had also noticed Jojo.

"What's your name?" Merlot asked, looking straight at him.

"Jojo," he said.

"Jojo the Yo-yo. I bet you can go up and down, around the world, and even walk my dog, if you need to."

Everyone laughed.

I had never seen Jojo at a loss for words, but Merlot had managed to silence him.

Just as Norm had been singled out at 801, Jojo had become Merlot's mark. Her dog skillfully wove in and out of her legs as Merlot did a soft-shoe number with a baton that she picked up from the side of the stage. Entertainment in Key West was definitely pet-friendly.

Eventually, she took off her top and threw it at Jojo, who held on to it with the same reverence he would show to Old Glory. Next, she tossed her tutu backstage, followed by a suggestive baton routine, where she mimicked having the climax of a lifetime.

She ended the show by removing her G-string, dangling it in front of Jojo, and then throwing it to another member of the audience.

"Hey, Milo. This one's for you, baby."

We all looked over to see the lucky guy and found another dwarf sitting at a table by himself at the left corner of the stage.

"Thanks, doll," he bantered back.

Jojo noticed he had competition, puckered his lips, and frowned like a neglected child.

Milo noticed Jojo's expression and gave him a salute with two fingers and then raised his glass to wish him good cheer, indicating it was all in good fun. It broke the ice because Jojo raised his glass back. Milo appeared to be in his forties, a few inches shorter than Jojo, and wore all black. He had an angular face with a fleshy nose that only added to his character.

After the show, Norm and my mother decided to go out for a few drinks. Raphael and I excused ourselves and went back to the house. I wanted him to see my place and now felt comfortable enough to have him there. Jojo stayed behind, wanting to meet Merlot backstage. As we excused ourselves and began our exit, I saw Milo wave Jojo over to his table to join him.

It had turned out to be an interesting evening. One I'd never forget and one I'm sure Norm was glad to have behind him.

23

Raphael had stayed at my house, and we were still up when Jojo came in close to 4:00 a.m. He had rented a scooter, which had a telltale sound. My mother slept in Norm's room and I had opened the sofa bed in the living room for Jojo with a note saying, "Think you'll be more comfortable down here. Will explain later. —Nick"

By eight o'clock, everyone was up and Norm, Raphael, Jojo, and I met by the pool. It didn't take much to figure out Jojo, relaxed and renewed, had spent the night with Merlot. I had recently undergone the same transformation, thanks to Raphael.

Jojo told us that Merlot had joined Milo and him at the table after the show. He also learned Milo was the owner of the pawnshop in town, was well connected, and had dealt with all types of people, from hookers to millionaires. Before landing here, he had owned a number of businesses.

Milo had known Merlot for years and always made a point of seeing her show when she was in town. From Jojo's tone, Milo and Merlot may have been more than friends at one time, and Jojo seemed jealous.

But Jojo was completely committed to his job and no matter what the distraction, he had come down to help us with the case.

Before Wanda left for the day, she made sure there was enough brewed coffee and fresh cinnamon rolls for all of us. She had been around police officers enough to know that those were staples.

"Did you guys enjoy the show?" Jojo asked.

Norm nodded then added, "I think I might have enjoyed it more without Wanda."

"I enjoyed it, too, but seeing a strip show with my mother..." I responded.

"It was fine," Raphael said. "Nothing unusual, but a good show."

"Merlot and I hit it off," Jojo said with a wide smile.

"We noticed," Norm said.

"She's quite a special lady," Jojo added.

"She is talented. Has she always been a stripper?" Norm asked.

There was a pause and then Jojo said, "She's worked numerous jobs, from political campaigns to being a madam, but said she was the happiest when she performed on stage. Since there weren't any other female strippers like her, she honed her skills and became a specialty act. She liked being her own boss. She married twice, both guys were deadbeats, so she's going to stay single for a while until Mr. Right comes along."

Jojo's eyes turned dreamy as he talked about her. He was smitten.

"She asked why I was down here. I just said I was on special assignment."

"That's good," Raphael said.

Norm and I knew that was a line Jojo often used when he needed to be discreet.

"I asked Merlot if she knew anything about the situation regarding Sho. Of course she had heard about it and was worried. I reassured Merlot that everything was being done to find her. What I haven't told you guys yet is that Sho probably was in the helicopter with Matt," Jojo said.

"How'd you find that out?" I asked.

"Connections."

"Who?" I continued.

"The 801 girls knew the pilot and key personnel in the hospital."

"Mercado?" Norm asked.

"He was rumored to be close to Sho," Jojo added.

I answered with an "umm."

"Mercado and Sho had been lovers for a while. Eventually, they had gone their separate ways, but Mercado still carried a torch for her," Jojo continued.

I looked over at Norm. That was the second time we heard about the two being lovers, first from Raphael and now through Jojo. Norm gave me a small nod.

"In the course of the evening, I also discovered Sho had been Commissioner Moss's ally," Jojo continued.

"Really?" Raphael said.

"Strange bedfellows," Norm said.

"Not when it comes to politics," Jojo answered. "Or anything else here, it seems."

I wondered if he was referring to Raphael and me, but I was probably being paranoid. Technically, I was working for the chief as a consultant and sleeping with him as a nymphomaniac.

"Moss was active in community politics," Raphael said, "especially when it came to gay issues. He was behind legislation that allowed all clubs—gay, straight, drag—to stay open without restrictions. My gaydar always went off when I was around him, but I never saw him with any guys other than his cronies, either at city meetings or public events. He certainly was considered gay friendly, though."

"Which would seem strange coming from Moss, right?" Jojo said.

"Unless he was in the closet," I said.

"He insisted it was important to keep the clubs on the cutting edge to attract tourists. The council bought it. Don't forget that without tourists, we'd be a ghost town," Raphael added.

"So it was all about bringing in money," Norm said.

"You would think," Jojo said.

"Was there more?" Raphael asked.

"You know he was married, had a family. He made sure to dot all the *i*'s and cross all the *t*'s," Jojo continued.

"I get the feeling there's more to this," I said.

I stood up, got the coffeepot, and refreshed everyone's cup. I was hoping there would be enough. Wanda had made two pots but we now had only half a pot left. I quickly brewed another. I also noticed there were crumbs all over the table, but this was not the time to clean up. I brought everyone a paper towel instead, hoping they'd get the hint. I also brought out another dozen cinnamon rolls, seeing the ones on the table had all disappeared.

"Merlot told me Moss had a secret gay lover. In fact, Moss and his lover had been meeting for years."

"You're shitting me," Norm said.

"My gaydar's still tuned in," Raphael added, gesturing an exclamatory *yes* by pulling his fist down.

"We're waiting, Jojo. Don't let us down now," I begged.

"That's just it. She didn't know who it was. Moss had sworn her to secrecy about the fact that he had a lover. He never even gave her a hint as to who it was."

"Raphael, any ideas?" I asked.

"I always wondered but never had any proof. Moss was slick."

"How about the other suicides?" I asked.

"She thought it was odd there had been so many recently, but had no clues as to why."

"Makes you wonder about Moss's suicide, doesn't it?" I said. The other men nodded seriously without offering any other insights. "Good work, Jojo," I added.

"Sounds like you were really busy last night," Norm said.

"It wasn't all work." Jojo gave us a wide smile.

"Sounds to me like you'll have to do some more investigating," I said.

"When duty calls," he said, and reached for another cinnamon roll.

24

Getting more information about the case unified the group.
Yes, each of us was involved in a personal relationship, each with
its own set of problems, but we were police officers first and for us
that was our passion, our obsession.

And then I thought of Raphael, who seemed to be the only one
among us who took his duties lightly. That bothered me. After all,
he was the chief of police. It was up to him to set an example for
his force.

THAT EVENING, Norm got a call from Patti. Since I was part of
the family now, he put the call on speakerphone.

"How are things going, Dad?" she asked.

"Slowly, but they're going," Norm said.

"Are you relaxing?"

"Not as much as we thought. We got pulled into a case," Norm
said.

"Dad, this was supposed to be a vacation, a reward for both
you and Nick."

"I know. But when a case calls, you know," Norm explained. "How are you and Mike? Mark and Johnny?"

"That's one of the reasons I'm calling. I was wondering how you'd feel about my bringing the boys down for a few days. The boys are off from January sixth through the thirteenth because of a teachers conference, and I don't know when we'll get a chance to get away again."

"Sure. You know you're always welcome," Norm said.

I knew he hadn't thought about his relationship with Wanda or maybe that was just it. Maybe he had and there really wasn't any relationship. All I knew was that it would be a complication, but I really looked forward to seeing Patti and the boys, since they always made me feel part of their family.

"What about Mike?" Norm asked. "We have loads of room here and there's a pool. He'd love it, too."

"He has to teach, papers to grade, new semester. You know how that goes, but he insists we go if it's all right with you and Nick." Norm looked up at me

"Of course it is. C'mon down."

WE HAD SOME unfinished business to deal with before Patti arrived with her boys.

Since learning about Matt's being transported to Miami, we knew it was important to ask Mercado some questions. I called and asked him to come in for questioning and he claimed he was interviewing interns and would prefer we come to the hospital. He wanted it on his turf, but it didn't matter as long as we got the job done.

We set the appointment for ten o'clock the following morning. When we got to the hospital, the lots were full except for a spot we found that required a bit of a walk, but it was in the high seventies with a calm wind. I couldn't get over the fact that the weather continued to remain the same each day. I wondered if the locals found it monotonous, but Norm and I were enjoying every second of it.

When we walked in, we went straight to the reception area and told Vivian (identified by a name tag with a smiley emoticon) we had an appointment with Dr. Mercado. She made a call and then said, "Dr. Mercado is in a meeting, but should be free in fifteen minutes. You can sit in the waiting room. I'll call you."

Norm and I looked at each other in disbelief, since we had identified ourselves as detectives and thought we would get more cooperation. Dr. Mercado certainly made sure he was in control.

We were finally cleared.

"The doctor will see you in his office on level three. If you take the elevators straight ahead of you and turn right, he'll be waiting for you. Be sure to get a visiting pass from the desk across the way." Then she looked over and saw there wasn't anyone there and said, "Never mind. Just go ahead. I'll vouch for you," and gave Norm a wink. She was eighty, if she was a day.

"I get all the lookers," Norm said.

"Must be that tan you're getting. Brings out your eyes," I said.

He tried to get close enough to give me a cuff as we walked to the elevators, but when we got on, there were a few other people so he had to behave.

In the elevator was a sign reminding staff that it was time to take the latest CPR training to be given on January fifteenth at 9:00 a.m. in the Coral Room. Certification was mandatory for every employee. I wondered if my recent mouth-to-mouth activities gave me automatic certification and smiled to myself.

Dr. Mercado was waiting for us when we got off the elevator.

"Thank you for accommodating me, gentlemen. It's been a whirlwind here. I've been tied up with interviews all morning and I have a few more this afternoon. I don't know where they all come from. Although I guess if I were an intern, I'd sure like to be able to do it here, so I can't blame them. But we only have slots for ten and we've had over two hundred applications."

Dr. Mercado had a lot to say. I hoped he'd be as forthcoming when it came to the transfer of Sho's husband, Matt.

The third floor had once been administrative offices, but because of lack of space, it now held some ICU patients and the doctor had to slide a key card through a slot and punch a series of numbers to enter. He motioned for us to follow.

The smell of antiseptic, various beeps from the monitors, and the groans of the patients welcomed us to the floor. Visitors attending the patients begged for attention from the nurses, since information was difficult to come by

Dr. Mercado led us to a small office at the end of a hallway. As he settled into his desk chair, I looked around the room. It was sparse and extremely neat. Behind his desk, a brag wall featured many photos of him with various celebrities of the Keys. The pictures were arranged in neat rows and in chronological order, based on what I could see of the fashions and hairstyles captured in each photo. Having OCD myself, I couldn't help but think Mercado had a touch of it. What amazed me the most was that when I entered I smelled lavender, a complete change from the hospital, and wondered where it came from. My eyes landed on a plug-in scent warmer in one of the outlets and I nodded to myself. I gave him points for lavender, since it was known for its calming properties.

"Welcome to my palace. It's the one place where I can get some peace and quiet. There are times I need to get away. I'm in charge of the hospital and it's a lot of responsibility."

"It is a lot of responsibility, Doctor. But according to your collection of commendations," gesturing to the wall, "you seem to be handling it well," I said, pandering to his ego.

"Well, I am the best."

Norm and I exchanged a glance. His bragging rights had amped into overdrive.

"You're a real saint, Doc," Norm said, trying to keep the sarcasm out of his voice, but Mercado was on a roll and just nodded.

"Enough about me. Why are *you* here? You're not sick, or are you?" He gave a laugh at his sad attempt at a joke.

"We're here to ask about Matt's transfer," Norm said.

"What about it?"

"Was it necessary?" I asked.

Mercado gave an insulted snort. "No. I decided a helicopter ride would improve his condition."

"Seriously. What was the reason?"

"Because he needed better care. *That's* the reason." There was a pause. Then he said, abruptly, "Are you questioning my medical decisions? I didn't invite you here to insult me. In fact, we're done. I'd like you to leave."

I looked at Norm, shocked. We both started to get up.

"I said NOW!"

We were standing. We had hit a nerve.

So much for calming lavender, I thought.

The doctor was standing too, glaring and breathing heavily. We left without saying another word. When we got to the car, I said, "That went well."

"You think?" Norm said. "I wonder if they're offering mandatory anger management classes at the hospital."

"He's beyond the Doctor Ego stage," I added. "Did you get a chance to see the photos on the wall behind him?"

"Not really."

"There were three of him with Sho, each from a different time period: early Queen Mother Pageant, Fantasy Fest, and New Year's Eve. The most notable was his being crowned King of Fantasy Fest by Sho. Another showed him smiling, standing next to Commissioner Moss at an AIDS benefit."

"Interesting," Norm said.

"Something went down with the helicopter transfer that Mercado doesn't want us to know about. Jojo's report that Sho had been transferred with Matt seemed the most likely." I went on to conclude, "I think we need to explore the back roads ourselves and see what we can find."

"Good idea."

"I'll ask Raphael if one of his rookies could be our guide. Maybe Brooks. The cop we met at Sandy's."

"Will he go along with it?"

"He better. I have some leverage now."

Norm smiled.

25

"We've never had so many people wanting to stay with us in Chicago," Norm said.

"Did Patti give you the weather report this morning?"

"Ten below."

"Where would you rather be?" I asked.

"That explains the two airbeds in my closet," Norm said.

"And mine. There's the sofa bed and futon in the living room, too. We can put everyone up. It'll just be family style."

Norm and I met Patti and the boys at the airport at 1:00 p.m. after grabbing a quick lunch. The boys were excited to see Grandpa and Uncle Nick and gave us hugs and kisses. It made my day. The weather was cooperating, with a breezy eighty-two degrees and low humidity.

"This is like summer," Johnny said.

"And it's like this all the time," I said.

"What about winter?" Mark asked.

"It might rain a little or get a bit cooler, but it never snows," I said.

"Is it true you have your own pool, Grandpa?" Johnny asked.

"Sure is. And you can go swimming as soon as we get there."

"How's Sho's case coming along?" Patti asked.

"We've still got a lot to do on it. Things move a lot slower here."

"Let me know if you need me."

Patti was a psychologist and had developed profiles for us before. When we entered the house, Nathan rushed up to greet the boys. They screamed with delight. When they bent down to pet him, the small, wriggling dog lavished each of them with pug kisses.

"When did you get him?" Johnny asked.

"He's not ours. He belongs to—"

"What's his name?" asked Mark.

Norm looked at me for help and I came to his rescue.

"My mom came to visit and she brought along her new dog. His name is Nathan. He's a pug." That satisfied their curiosity.

I gave them a quick tour and showed them where they'd be staying. I had already talked to Jojo, and he and I would take the sofa and futon downstairs. I gave Patti and the boys my room upstairs. After they changed into shorts and T-shirts, I took them out to see the grounds.

Patti walked around the pool, amazed at the beauty of the two juxtaposed bodies of water. Wanda was sitting in a chaise wearing a white bikini, reading a copy of *Cosmopolitan*.

The boys startled her and she turned and looked up to see what was going on.

"Hello, I'm Wanda, Nick's mother. Your grandpa showed me your pictures and said you'd be coming in."

"Hi, I'm Norm's daughter, Patti, and these are my two boys, Johnny and Mark. We spoke briefly when I gave you my dad's address."

"Thanks again. That was so helpful. How nice to meet all of you," Wanda said.

"Are you Grandpa's girlfriend?"

"Johnny, that's not polite," Patti said.

I waited to see what my mother or Norm would say next as the conversation came to a standstill.

"That's something your grandpa needs to answer," Wanda said.

"She is my friend," Norm said.

"And my mother," I said.

"I got it. She can be our grand friend," Johnny said.

Wanda laughed. "Yes, I'd like that. What do you say, Norm?"

"I'd say the boys nailed it."

We all gave a sigh of relief.

With that, the boys took off running through the yard with Nathan trying to catch them.

"I see Nathan likes them."

"They keep begging for a puppy, but we're just too busy to have one right now."

"He's cute but requires a lot of attention. I had no idea. Be sure you're ready before you get one."

I watched the exchange and saw that Wanda and Patti were sizing each other up. This could be either a complete disaster or a blessing. I prayed for the latter.

"First one into the pool gets ice cream for lunch," I said.

"We'll see about that, Uncle Nick," Patti said, smiling. "And, boys, I want you to listen to what I have to say. Mark, Johnny, get over here."

They were so busy playing with Nathan, they didn't hear her.

"I said, *now.*"

I remembered that tone of voice and knew it meant business. I had to fight the urge to line up with them.

They both came running up to their mom and stood close to each other like soldiers waiting for their orders.

"I know you both like to swim and that you've taken lessons. But I want you to listen to me very carefully. Under no circumstances are you to be in the pool or go to the beach without an adult. Is that understood?"

"Yes, Mom," Johnny said.

"Um-hmm," Mark said.

Nathan started tugging at Johnny's sock. He wanted to keep playing. Wanda just shook her head, enjoying the show.

"Can Nathan come into the pool?" Johnny asked.

"Nathan isn't much of a swimmer," I said. "Some dogs are and some aren't. He can swim if he has to, but he doesn't like the water."

"Aww," Johnny said.

"I want to let you know that although you're here on vacation, Uncle Nick and I might not be around a lot. We're busy on a couple of cases, so feel free to have a good time and we'll join you when we can."

They nodded and went into the house with Patti, changed into their swimsuits, came out, and jumped into the pool. As boys often do, they enjoyed splashing each other, trying to drown each other, and trying to swim through each other's legs. Patti and my mom watched from the sidelines, enjoying the show.

Norm pulled me aside and said, "You prepared for meeting with the detectives?"

"Let's see what they've got and take it from there."

"Sounds good."

Patti decided it was time for her sons to come out of the water. There were a lot of cries of, "Just another ten minutes. Please, Mom, please," but all to no avail. When they saw Nathan waiting to play with them, they got excited again.

I wasn't sure they heard or cared, but when I said, "If your mom says it's okay, we'll go to Mallory Square later. It's like going to Navy Pier in Chicago, but it's all outside. There's a special show there we can all enjoy. It's put on by the Catman."

I had captured their attention. They were all ears.

"Like Batman?" Johnny asked.

"Or Superman?" Mark asked.

"If I'm good, can I come?" Wanda asked.

We all turned to look at her. I knew she was upset because she wasn't getting more attention.

Patti exchanged a look with her father. My mother was being a Catwoman. I went and hugged her anyway.

"Mom, you know you're loved," I whispered into her ear.

"Thank you, *Nickala*. I was beginning to think you forgot you had a mother."

"You'll always be my mother." I smiled. I had almost forgotten her guilt trips.

Jojo came through the French doors, bleary-eyed and looking hung over. The boys froze in place when they saw him.

Johnny tugged the bottom of my shirt and gestured for me to bend down. He whispered into my ear, "Who's that?"

"That's Jojo. He works with us."

"Why is he so small?" Mark asked.

Patti interjected. "It's not polite to whisper in front of someone, boys. Nick, why don't you introduce your friend to us?"

"Jojo, this is Patti, Norm's daughter."

"Pleased to meet you, Jojo. I've heard a lot about you."

"Don't believe everything you hear unless it's good, of course," he said, and laughed.

"And these are my two boys, Johnny and Mark."

Jojo walked up to them and shook their hands and said how happy he was to meet them.

They stood in place staring at him.

"Can I ask you something? I was wondering about your—" Mark said, still eyeing Jojo.

Patti broke in. "Boys, remember: respect and acceptance."

Mark looked at his mom, then Jojo, and grew quiet.

"Oh," Johnny broke in, "I have a question."

"Yes?" Jojo said patiently.

"Do you like to swim?"

"Oh, yes. It's one of my favorite things. Do you?"

"Oh, yeah. Will you swim with us later?" and then Nathan barked, wanting to play. "Nice to meet you, Mr. Jojo," they yelled as they ran off chasing Nathan. A few chickens had wandered into the yard, so they all got involved, and there was a lot of clucking and barking. Nathan never caught the chickens but he certainly enjoyed chasing them.

We told Jojo we were off to the station to talk to the detectives about the suicides and we wanted him to join us. I also mentioned our plan to comb the back roads near the hospital.

"Sure. I have something to do but I'll see you later."

Jojo looked like a real player as he jumped on his scooter and rode off.

26

"Do you think Patti and Wanda will be okay?" Norm asked.

I had wondered the same thing, but for now, there wasn't anything we could do about it. Patti was a protective daughter but also an open thinker, and I'm sure she wanted only the best for her father.

"Who's to say?" I said. "We have work to do."

"Women," Norm said, shaking his head.

"Men," I said.

We both laughed.

It was time to get more information on the suicides. We had called to make sure Warren and Bridges, the detectives who worked the cases, would be there, and set off for the station.

On our way there, I thought about my mother and what she was thinking. I knew her well enough to know something was wrong, other than Patti's being there. She had always felt excluded and wanted me to be with her as much as possible, more so since my father died. I had avoided her smothering, but not without paying a price. I could see she was doing the same thing to Norm.

"How are things going with you and my mom?" I asked.

Norm paused as if thinking whether it was a good idea to talk about their relationship but decided it was okay.

"Little rocky right now," Norm said.

"Because you won't let her get involved in the case?"

"Yeah, that and..." he trailed off.

"She can be difficult but she means well," I said. "I love her. She's my mother, but whatever happens to the two of you is your business."

"I know that. She's a good woman, but she wants it *all*, right now, and I'm not sure I'm ready."

"Have you told her that?"

"It's a tricky situation, ya know. I'd like to but I don't want to fight with her. We're enjoying each other but I don't know if it's because we're here. This place isn't Chicago."

"Toto, we're not in Kansas anymore."

HQ was only five minutes away from our place, but I noticed Norm had decided to ride along the beach, giving us a little more time. We both wanted to work the case but we also wanted to discuss our romantic entanglements.

"How about you and Raphael?"

"He's a handful," and then I realized what I said and hoped Norm wouldn't come back with one of his smart-ass remarks.

But he realized we were being serious, and he kept silent. I was relieved.

"He's used to getting his way."

"So is she," he said, referring to my mother. "You know I'm here for you, bud. Always."

My eyes filled with tears and I started to answer but nothing came out. I was reminded of Darren and that was what he would say to me. I waited a minute because I wanted him to hear it. "The same for you, Norm."

Neither of us looked at each other.

"Good talk," Norm said.

27

We walked up to the desk sergeant. She was in her fifties, skinny as a stick, and kept her hair back in an unruly ponytail.

"Detectives Malone and Scott here. We'd like to speak to Detectives Warren and Bridges. We called ahead."

She looked us up and down, nodded, aware we were working with them, and said, "I'm Sergeant Ellinger." She picked up the phone and announced our arrival.

Detective Warren, fortyish, red-tomato face with a pear-shaped body, came up and introduced himself.

"Good to meet you. The chief said you'd be wanting to talk to us. Follow me back. I'll introduce you to Bridges."

The station was laid out as a rectangle with gray walls, long corridors, and an open space with cubicles for the various officers. It had been redone about ten years ago, due to heavy water damage after Hurricane Wilma. The city paid for a face-lift but it came out looking like a budget nip-and-tuck held together by a few stitches. The space resembled our station in Chicago, only smaller.

Bridges was sitting at a steel desk, writing a report. He had thick brown hair, an oval face, and a straight nose. He needed a shave. When he stood up, he looked like he could have been a defensive guard for the Heat, standing at six one and weighing in at 210 pounds.

"Ya wanna stay here or go out someplace?" Bridges said.

"We can offer you bad coffee," Warren said.

"We have the same brand at our place. We'll stay," Norm said.

"We both like it black," I said.

Warren led us to one of the small conference rooms that probably served as a multipurpose interview and meeting room. There weren't any pictures on the walls and the four wooden chairs were scattered around the room. Warren made small talk as we waited for Bridges to return.

"You enjoying your stay?"

"It's one hell of a place," Norm said.

"Yup," he said.

That was as far as we got before Bridges returned with the coffees.

"Sorry, guys. There were donuts, but you know how fast those go."

We took our places. Norm and I sat next to each other, and Warren and Bridges sat across from us.

"So what can we do for you?" Bridges asked.

"The chief told us you two worked the suicides, and we had a few questions."

"Ask away," Warren said.

"First, any word on security footage on Moss?" I asked.

"Someone erased it," Warren said.

"How could that happen?" Norm asked.

"Inside job. Someone knew someone and called in a favor," Bridges answered.

"Jeez," I said.

"Don't forget, it was New Year's Day. It wouldn't take much to get in there."

"So we're counting this a murder, not a suicide?" I said.

"Not necessarily. But someone was in there and didn't want us to see anything," Warren said.

"Okay. How about tox screen?" Norm asked.

"We're talking about less than a week ago. It'll take another two weeks at least," Warren said.

"Or two months," Bridges added.

"Or two years," Warren said, and they both laughed.

"Isn't there some way you could put a rush on it? Call someone?" I asked.

"Nope. Not the way it works here. You're on Key West time. Getting a handyman to come out to fix a broken window can take a week," Warren said.

"And that's if he's a relative," Bridges added, and they both laughed again.

I looked at Norm and wondered how anything got done here.

Then there was a knock on the door and Sergeant Ellinger announced, "Jojo's here."

"Great, send him in," Bridges said.

Jojo entered and they introduced themselves. While Warren was getting a chair, I filled Jojo in on the latest in Moss's case. Jojo often caught things we missed.

"Your ME said there were four suicides and five mysterious deaths during the past year. A lot for you guys, right?" Norm asked when Warren returned.

"Surprisingly."

"More than usual."

"Let's go over the last four," I said.

Warren had pulled all the files, so we had them in front of us. He put them in order by month so the most recent was first.

Bridges took over the presentation. "Tom Moss, married, fifty, two kids, commissioner for four years, generally a jerk but got things done when necessary. Too many enemies to count."

Norm and I looked at each other. Each file looked flat, the paperwork in each sparse. Had they considered each a slam-dunk suicide as far as working the case? It was up to all of us to start thinking of these vics as murdered. There was a killer out there, a dangerous one.

"Then we come to Patrick Knowles, a single, thirty-five-year-old male, found in his rented efficiency, hanging in his kitchen. He was a DEA officer assigned to this region. Regular guy. Gay. No known priors and was a loner."

Norm started to rub his right finger around the edge of his coffee cup. I knew he was taking it all in, but he was also upset. Since we often thought alike, I felt we were hearing a litany of facts that could be found in an obituary, rather than anything in workups that had been done on the vics.

"The next one was Sean Baxter, a fifty-five-year-old Democratic congressman from Miami: good reputation, liked by his constituents, reelected twice, thinking about a presidential run. He was a family man, wife, two young kids, nine and eleven. Had a vacation place here in the Casa Marina. His wife found him hanging in the bedroom. Her report is in the file."

"So far, all of them were officials," I said.

Bridges nodded and then said, "Noted." Norm and I exchanged a glance.

"The next was Junior Turino, an undercover cop, one of ours, who worked in Narco as a dealer. Thirty two years old, single, Caucasian. He liked to paddleboard, kayak, and run marathons. His friends described him as outgoing, well liked, and comical. He was found hanging from a light fixture in his bedroom the day after placing second in a 10K triathlon."

"Did they all leave notes?" Jojo asked.

"Yeah. Nothing unusual," Warren said.

"Can I take a look?"

"Sure."

Jojo studied the notes and then said, "Would it be normal for Moss to use the word *a-holes*?"

The question made them stop for a minute.

"He had a filthy mouth," Warren said.

"*F* this, *F* that. No, he would have used *assholes*," Bridges said.

"He could have been telling us something," Nick added.

"That he wasn't being himself," Norm added. "Maybe he was forced to write the letter."

"Possible," Bridges conceded. "Let's finish up and come back to that."

Warren took over and was ready to go over the other five deaths when there was a knock on the door. A delivery boy brought in three piping-hot pizzas and two large bottles of Coke.

"Whoa," said Bridges.

"How'd this happen?" Warren asked.

Norm, Jojo, and I shrugged. None of us had anything to do with it, although it was something our team would have done back in Chicago.

Warren and Bridges looked at each other as serious as a terrorist alert, and Warren asked, "All right, which one of you's fucking the chief?"

I felt my heart speed up and wished for Harry Potter's invisibility cloak.

Without skipping a beat, Norm said, "I am," and then like a football team captain, motioned for everyone to move in for a huddle. "It's his way of apologizing because, well, he's..." Norm held his forefinger and thumb about an inch apart and brought them closer to his face to indicate that the chief had a tiny dick.

We all laughed. I was glad I was still sunburned so they wouldn't see me blush. We all clapped Norm on the back and greedily dove into the pizzas. It was the perfect time for a break. I smiled, knowing otherwise about the chief.

It was almost 5:00 p.m. and normally the three of us would have stayed on to continue working the case, but Norm and I had commitments at home. Jojo offered to stay behind to work with the detectives. He wasn't interested in seeing the Catman. His only civilian interest on the island was Merlot.

As we were leaving, I ran into Raphael in the hall.

"Thanks for the pizza. Appreciated it."

"You're welcome."

By the look in his eye, I knew what he wanted and saw this as the perfect opportunity.

"Raphael, I wondered if we could work with Officer Brooks, your rookie, to search for evidence on the back roads." I gave him a sexy smile, hoping it would give me some leverage. I wanted Brooks because he was new and might not have the nonchalant attitude of some of the seasoned officers.

"You mean D.J.?"

I nodded.

"I think it's a waste of time, but if it will make you feel better, sure. He's a Conch, so he knows the island."

"Thanks. I promise I'll show you my appreciation next time we're together."

He gave a knowing grin and said, "Get out of here before I handcuff you."

"Save that thought," I said, "for later."

28

CATMAN

Mallory Square was located on the west side of the island at the end of Duval and Front Streets. Each night, hundreds of tourists and locals alike would head toward the pier to watch the spectacular sunsets, a tradition that had been going on for years. The march to the pier resembled lemmings going toward a cliff and began an hour or two before the event. Many vendors set themselves up to showcase their wares or their acts in hopes of making money, and the locals and visitors alike were happy to take the bait. They were the modern-day pirates hoping to strike treasure. One of the most successful, and the one we were going to see, was the Catman.

Raphael pled work, so he was out. Wanda claimed allergies to cats, so she was out. That left Patti, the two boys, Norm, and me. Personally, I thought it worked out well for all.

The pier's many attractions included Spiderman, a juggler, psychics, and assorted artists and cotton-candy makers. A crowd had already started to assemble for the Catman, but we were lucky to find a spot near the front so that the boys had a clear view of the show. The entertainer was so popular he did two shows, but the one before sunset drew the larger crowd. No one competed with the sunset. They were sure to lose.

I knew from experience that any area that appealed to the public also drew its share of drug dealers and shady types. I wondered how many of them were already in place to make their deals.

"I think Jojo's on to something with the note," I said.

"I do too. It's our first good lead. If the perp's a serial killer, what do the vics have in common?"

"I didn't see a pattern when we met with the detectives, but Jojo's good at connecting the dots."

Johnny tugged at my shirt. "When does it start?"

"Soon." My conversation with Norm would have to wait.

The Catman's act was performed by Pierre on the pier. The entertainer wore his bushy white-and-brown hair in an Afro. He sported an odd beige-striped tux topcoat and baggy black pants to heighten the image of his being the ringmaster at a circus. The effect was eclectic, theatrical, hip.

"Welcome, smudies and lodgkies, to the one and only smell-of-licorice show of the Catman."

People looked around at each other wondering what he had just said, but that was the point. He spoke gibberish, mixed with some English and a few French words. He claimed to have come to Key West from Paris, where he was the main attraction at the Eiffel Tower. Rumor had it he was a Conch who had spent most of his time as a tour guide, but he used his imagination and his cleverness to turn what others might consider crazy into a "show that couldn't be missed."

"Does he have lions?" Johnny asked.

"I don't see any, do you?" Norm said.

"Just cages, hoops, and tightropes," Mark said.

"Maybe they're small lions," I said, making the boys look at each other, wondering if it were true.

Patti smiled at me, enjoying being with all of us in such a beautiful setting. She didn't care what we saw. Many sailboats and yachts were docked in the harbor, and as the sun began to set, a golden glow made the whole scene magical.

"Behold, my first schudle. Mook will now come out and walk this narrow tightrope for me."

He snapped his fingers and an ordinary gray-striped cat came out of its cage and walked across the rope and then jumped down and into another cage. The audience clapped and the boys watched in awe. The truth was, everyone did.

"Marvelous. Schpectle, supercalifragili. Sing with me, boys and girls."

The boys joined in, singing the popular song from *Mary Poppins*. "Super."

"My next kitty will perform *wunderbar*, delumptious feats."

He made a noise, combining a whistle and a cluck of his tongue that made him sound like a rooster with laryngitis. A black cat jumped out of her cage and onto his shoulder.

"Lucette is from a very special place called Lapalaluza. When I found her, she was a scrawny, unfed kitten with no one but me. I schmoozed her, cushelled her, and now she loves me."

On cue, she nuzzled his cheek and meowed. He had trained them to perform and they listened. As far as I was concerned, those were incredible tricks for cats. I didn't know any that listened to anyone.

The show continued until there were six cats of various sizes, shapes, and colors performing numerous tricks for the Catman.

He then asked for two assistants and chose two avid fans: Johnny and Mark. He asked each of them to hold a hoop and stand at opposite ends of his stage, while he held a flaming hoop and stood in the middle.

"Mushie, Alexa, Mook, Lucette, Beanush, and Groosh, begin." Three cats were stationed on one crate behind Mark, and three were on a crate behind Johnny. Mushie, then Alexa, then Mook jumped from the top of one crate onto Mark's shoulder and then through his hoop onto a tightrope, then through the Catman's flaming hoop, back onto the wire and through Johnny's hoop. Lucette, Beanush, and Groosh had begun at the same time on Johnny's end, doing the same tricks onto a parallel tightrope, ending on the crate nearest Mark. The act gave the feeling of flying cats everywhere.

I joined the rest of the crowd and clapped loudly at the finale, since it was unlike anything any of us had ever seen.

The boys were given free tickets to the next show but since all the shows were free, it seemed pointless. They were also instructed to hand out postcards to those around them.

"Ladies and smutts, please realize I am but a poor entertainer who depends on your tips to feed my performers and myself." All spoken in the Queen's English. "For a mere twenty five dollars, I also have T-shirts of all sizes. My two assistants will get a five-dollar discount on theirs."

Catman had placed an open crate for the tips a few feet away from where he stood. Most of the audience came up, and I guessed he probably made $100 to $150 for his half-hour show. If he did the same at the next show, he was clearing nearly $300 a day for an hour's work. He might be strange, but he was making a bundle, and he didn't have to put it in a blind trust.

Norm and I were already digging into our wallets. The boys had to have a T-shirt of the Catman of Key West. Johnny picked out a blue one with Lucette, the black cat, jumping through the ring of fire. Mark chose a black shirt with Groosh, a white cat, doing the same trick.

"Can we wear them? Please, please, please."

Patti acquiesced. They had been fearless assistants.

Once the show was over, we moved farther away from the action to watch the sunset in peace. The bright-orange globe slowly slipped into the water, and a rare phenomenon occurred. An intense green ray, lasting only two seconds, shot out from the fiery orb. The audience oohed and clapped in appreciation. We had been treated to not one but two shows, the latter being even more phenomenal.

"Boys, you were lucky. That only happens once in a million times and you were here to see it," I said

"Once in a million?" Patti questioned.

"Maybe once in a thousand," Norm said, "but definitely not very often."

"It's very rare," I added.

Patti liked to keep things real when Norm and I were together with the boys. Once she said, "I sometimes wonder which pair of you, my boys or the two of you, are the children."

The happiness they gave me made everything else seem insignificant in comparison.

29

By the time we had eaten and found our way back home, it was nearly 9:00 p.m. The boys got ready for bed and were soon fast asleep.

"Did you have a nice time?" Wanda asked.

"Oh yes," Patti said. "I wish you had come or at least joined us for dinner—"

"I'm sure it was entertaining," Wanda interrupted. "Norm, do you think you can rub my shoulders? I seem to have developed a knot that just won't go away."

If it wasn't clear what was going on before, Wanda made a point of drawing a spotlight on Norm and her.

"Let's all go sit outside by the pool. It's such a beautiful night," I suggested.

"I prefer to stay here. I'm not feeling up to par," Wanda said.

"Can I make anyone a drink?" I asked.

Norm ordered a double, my mom ordered her usual, Patti wanted a rum and Coke, and I decided to have an iced tea for a change.

My phone dinged, indicating an incoming message.

It was from Jojo.

> Just leaving station. Some progress with profiles. Have more questions. Need psychologicals. Have a theory.

I relayed the message to Norm.

"I can't believe they didn't get psychs on these guys. That would have been a natural back at our station," Norm replied.

"I know what you're saying, Norm. Are you thinking cover-up?"

"Maybe, but what does that say about Perez?"

I didn't have an answer and yet he had a point. Seeing that each case only had a page or two, not much had been done in the way of reports. There were brief histories and an assumption that each had committed suicide. Open-and-shut cases, which were rapidly becoming cold ones. No one ever considered they were murdered until Tom Moss turned up dead.

"Why didn't Perez get more information on these guys?" The slam-dunk suicide theory popped up again.

"By the time they find someone to do it and follow up on all the interviews again, it will be another six months to a year down here," Norm said.

"I know," I said, quietly.

"Patti, you've done some profiles for us. Would you mind taking a look at what Jojo's working on?" Norm asked.

"Not at all."

Wanda immediately pushed Norm's hands away from her neck, where he had been massaging her.

"Did I hear this right?" she asked.

"What?" Norm said.

"Did you just ask your daughter to help you on the case?"

I saw where this was going and knew Norm was in big trouble. What my mom didn't know was that Patti was a trained psychologist and had studied profiling.

"Mom, Patti does this for a living. She's a psychologist."

If she heard me, she refused to register it. I knew her tirades and felt we were in for a doozy.

"When I try to help, I'm told to stop meddling, or you can't share confidential information, or you're consulting for the chief. One bullshit reason after another," she said as her voice amped up in volume. "Finally, I'm told to go shopping."

"Wanda, it's not like that. Listen to me."

"I don't have to do it." Patti tried to intervene, hoping to stop the argument before it went any further. But her comment went unheard. Voices had begun to escalate even more.

"No, you listen to me. What I think doesn't matter to you."

"It does. It's not what you think," Norm tried to explain.

"Now you're going to tell me I'm not allowed to think what I want, either."

She had had enough exclusion. Patti and the boys were getting attention, I'd deserted her for their family, and now Patti was being asked to be part of the case.

"I'm good enough to sleep with, but not important enough to be included in your casework. Go fuck yourself, Norm."

Wanda got up, picked up her drink, and threw it in Norm's face.

"Wanda, that was completely uncalled for. I've worked for the Chicago police department before. It has nothing to do with my relationship with my dad," Patti said.

Wanda ignored her. Patti went into the kitchen to get a towel for her father.

As she wiped the drink off her dad's face, she said, "How rude, Wanda. Who do you think you are, anyway?"

Norm got up and tried to grab Wanda's arm to stop her from leaving the room.

"Get your hands off me. I'm leaving. I know when I'm not wanted anymore."

"Mom, please. Can't you wait until morning? We can talk about it then."

"This is between Norm and me. Stay out of it."

She marched to her room, and you could hear her opening and slamming drawers as she packed up her things.

Norm got up to go to her and I stopped him. Nothing he said would change her mind. I had seen her blowups before, and it was best if he stayed away.

Patti looked up. "Dad, I'm sorry she did that to you."

"Don't worry, honey. I can handle this. She's feeling left out and the rest is stuff she and I need to work out," Norm continued. "You've worked with us before. You'll get us the information we need quickly and that's what we need right now."

This could be the end of Norm and Wanda, but to Norm, the case was king. It came before anything else.

From the back of the house we could hear, "Could you send a cab to Hidden Sands Resort, immediately?" There was a pause. "No, I don't know the address. It's next to Louie's Backyard. I'd think you'd know that. Thank you."

The boys, camping on airbeds upstairs, slept through this, but Nathan came downstairs and began barking and running back and forth, whimpering. He didn't know what was going on.

Within minutes, the cab pulled up and honked its horn.

Wanda walked into the living room with her luggage. She bent down, picked up Nathan, and kissed him. "Sorry, dear. You're a good boy. Momma's going to miss you."

She handed him to Norm.

"Consider this my going-away gift. He'll be happier with you and Patti's boys. You made it clear they know how to love better, too. We all make choices. You made yours and I made mine. Now we must live with them."

Norm jerked his head back as if the words were a slap in the face.

"*Nickala*, would you help bring my luggage to the cab?"

I picked up her suitcase and followed behind like an obedient bellboy. She gave me a quick hug and kiss.

"Don't forget, you only have one mother. I'm taking the next plane back to Chicago. Call me." And with that she got in the cab and was off to the airport.

Norm and I sat in the living room, speechless. Just a few hours ago we were having a great time enjoying the sunset and laughing with the boys, and now my mother had created a scene and left.

My mom's quick exit reminded me of Darren's sudden departure. He had been murdered and taken away from me for no apparent reason. My mother had her reasons, as ridiculous as they seemed, but it left me with the emptiness I felt when I saw the ambulance pull away with Darren's body. Whoever said it wouldn't hurt as much after a year was wrong. There were times, like now, where I felt my heart had been ripped out of my body.

I picked up Nathan, said good night to Norm and Patti, and headed for my room. I couldn't handle anything else this evening. I looked back for a moment. Norm stood quietly, shoulders slumped, a sad, confused look on his face.

30

When the phone rang and Norm saw it was Wanda, he hesi-
tated in picking it up. He let it go to voicemail.

"It's Wanda. I want to apologize for last night. I don't know what
got into me. I like you, Norm. We had such a good time. A much
better time than I ever thought possible. I still have feelings for
you. Please forgive me."

Her voice was a little shaky with emotion. "But I'm not sure
about our future because of Nicky. I'm his mother and you're his
partner. We both love him in different ways, and I appreciate how
you protect him like an older brother he never had."

Now her voice was quieter, like she was getting to what made
her call. "I need time to sort all this out. I'd hope we could be
friends. I hope that's possible. Norm, you're a very special man. I'm
glad we've had what we did."

Norm wished she were here so he could wrap his arms around
her and take her to bed. He wanted to comfort and assure her that
everything would be okay. He still cared for her.

"All right. Take care of yourself and, of course, Nicky. Thanks
for understanding."

He still cared for her but didn't understand her. He still didn't know why she got that upset and created such a scene. The woman had issues, but who didn't? He didn't want to lose her.

Norm didn't delete the message. He just stood thinking. His feelings for her were strong, but he didn't know how they'd play out. The only thing he knew for sure was that they both wanted to do the right thing for Nick.

31

When I woke the next morning, I found Norm sitting alone at the kitchen table, drinking coffee. Considering what occurred last night with my mom, he seemed to be holding up, but he could hide his feelings well.

"Your mom called this morning."

"Anything you want to talk about?"

"No, it's all good."

I knew it wasn't, but that was the end of the conversation. If at some point he wanted to tell me about it, he would. I made another pot of coffee. I had slept poorly. I hoped I wasn't getting into one of my insomnia states. When I felt overwhelmed, that often happened. I was starting to handle it by having an occasional stiff drink before going to bed. I knew it wasn't a good idea, but it worked.

With my mother gone, there was one less distraction, and Norm and I could concentrate on the case. I felt bad for Norm, but like most things with Norm, he lived in the moment and seemed fine.

Raphael had given me the go-ahead to work with D.J. to comb the back roads, and I thought we should take advantage of the situation before Raphael changed his mind.

I called the station and asked to speak to D.J. With a few clicks and a slight pause, he came on the line.

"Brooks here."

"Officer Brooks, this is Detective Scott. I've spoken to Chief Perez about you helping us search for evidence of Sho's disappearance. Has he briefed you about it?"

"Yes, he did. I'd be glad to help. When?"

"My partner and I are free now if you are."

"I am. Where did you want to search?"

"The back roads near the hospital. I have a suspicion the EMTs may have dropped Sho off in the area."

"Sure. I could meet you at the hospital entrance."

"That's perfect. How about noon?"

"Perfect. You can't miss me. I'm big, tall, and black," he chuckled. "You know, the Quota Cop."

After being at HQ, I knew he was the only African American on the force. "See you soon." I already liked his honest sense of humor.

Brooks was a pleasure to work with. He wanted to help and thought it was a good idea. Even more important, he took his job seriously. Norm and I joined him in his car, and he led us to the first road he thought could be a possibility.

"There are a lot of side paths around here and once we get to the end of the road, we'll need to hoof it. I brought along some bug spray. If you don't use it, you'll be eaten alive."

He drove us along the road at a slow pace so we wouldn't miss anything that might look suspicious. He had been through here before; he avoided the rough parts of the road. Finally, he had to stop, and we followed him on foot as he led the way.

I let D.J. get farther ahead of us, out of earshot.

"Norm, I've known my mother for a long time and I've never seen her happier than I did with you."

"We had some good times."

"I hope none of this has to do with me."

"Naw. It's all about the two of us." Norm avoided looking at me, a sign it wasn't so. "However it goes down, you had nothing to do with it."

"Are you still going to see her?"

"We both need to figure that out."

"How are you guys holding up?" D.J. asked.

"Fine," I said, lying through my teeth. Norm and I were both soaked from the heat and humidity. Luckily, D.J. had brought along some bottled water so we could keep hydrated.

After an hour, he suggested returning to the car and trying another road farther away from the hospital and one only the locals knew.

As we followed the same routine, we kept our eyes peeled for anything that would give us a clue to Sho's disappearance.

"We can come back another time, Detectives. I know this is brutal. I'm used to this weather and it's getting to me, so you tell me when."

"Thanks, D.J.," I said. Norm looked close to collapsing.

"Let's give it another half hour," Norm said stoically.

We pushed on and just as we were coming to the end of our time, D.J. spotted something glimmering in the dirt. He shined his light on it, the beam cutting through the shadows, and leaned down for a look.

"Come here, guys. It's covered with a lot of crud, but everyone remembers Sho's dress, and this could be a piece of it."

We rushed over to take a look, and although it had turned a muddy gray, a small section sparkled like a treasure.

"D.J.," I said, "I know you're supposed to call in and have them come to the scene, but I have this plastic bag that I could use to pick it up, and we could leave a red flag to designate the area if you're okay with that."

He thought about it for a minute and said, "My job was to lead you through the brush, but I wasn't instructed to look for evidence. You two are special consultants, so I am technically under your command."

Norm and I looked at each other and smiled. We both liked how D.J. was playing it. He knew if he left it to the chief, there was no telling what might happen. If he let us do our job, it might prove to be a valuable clue. He was walking a thin line and he was willing to take that chance.

After securing the evidence, he brought us back to our car. We parted ways and D.J. said, "I hope I've been of help today, Detectives."

"More than you know, D.J."

He gave us a smile.

The piece of fabric was the first solid clue we had, but it would have to wait until I could show it to Jojo. If nothing else, it proved Sho had been here.

When we got back to the resort, Norm and I ran to our respective showers to clean up. Our afternoon had been exhausting but productive. It was nearly 5:00 p.m. and the house was empty. Patti had likely taken the boys out to see sights, and Jojo could be following a lead. I could grab a quick nap before dinner. Norm and I were so exhausted, we both slept through the night.

32

The next day I assessed where we were with the cases. Our discovery of a piece of Sho's dress could provide us with possible DNA and lead us to our suspect.

As far as the hangings, the possible clue in Tom Moss's note could prove he didn't act alone.

Through Patti's evaluations, Norm and I had determined that the last four suicides were questionable. We still didn't have a motive, but with Patti's help we might get some clues. When looking deeper into Moss's past, we learned he owned six bars, two hotels, and three restaurants on Duval Street. He worked as a commissioner, so it was doubtful he maintained his opulent lifestyle that way. He came from old money, so he probably had assets, but still, to own such prime property on Duval took a lot. We needed more information and the Bubba system seemed impenetrable.

Bubbas hung together no matter what. They were compared to the Good Ole Boys network. Money deals were often made with the Key West briefcase—in other words, cash. Houses not listed on the market had new owners. It was unwritten and unsaid, a conspiracy of silence. We needed access to privileged information that seemed sealed by Bubbas.

One thing I learned on the island was that word spread fast through a people's network the locals called the Coconut Telegraph. Rose Richards, TV anchor for *America Today*, was known to come to vacation here often, and it just so happened she was here now. If I could find a way to reach her, maybe I could convince her to do a special with me concerning the suicides. Tina, host of *Keys, Please*, owed me one for doing her show. We could start with an intro about suicides and depression, then name the four victims we were recently profiling, and then open the show to call-ins to elicit information.

I'd need to run it by Raphael but I didn't see why he'd protest. If anything, it would help him solve the case, if that was what he wanted to do. I was beginning to have my doubts. I hadn't heard from him last night and wondered what that was about, but I decided to shelve it for now. I was still recovering from my mother's sudden departure and the memories of Darren it triggered.

Once Norm was up, I laid out my plan. He was all in but a little skeptical.

"How are you going to find Rose Richards?" Norm asked. "I'm sure she's guarding her privacy."

"That's true, but there's a network of people who make it their business to know where people are staying. Tina owes me big-time and I plan to start there. Having a show with Rose would be a coup for her and she knows it. She's a very ambitious newscaster, as you saw. And if she doesn't have any leads, I can guarantee you, her producer will."

Norm was walking around wearing only boxers and flip-flops. His way of adapting to the new climate and to its insect and lizard inhabitants was to make sure he didn't step on them with his bare feet. What differed here from the Midwest was that there were a number of unknown bugs and lizards that seemed impossible to control. The law of survival was: geckos ate mosquitos, iguanas ate vegetation, and the iguanas multiplied and ruled the land. Worst of all were the dreaded palmettos, a fancy word for flying roaches. Many residents had their houses routinely sprayed or bug bombed. Neither Norm nor I appreciated these critters, but it was a small price to pay. After all, they were all here first.

The locals took it all in stride, many buying icons of the lizards to hang on their fences to ward off bugs. I'd have to find one. I was beginning to think like a local, and that could be to my advantage in helping to solve the case. I hoped there was some sort of debriefing once I left the island, because no one would understand me back on the mainland.

At 9:00 a.m., I called Tina to ask her about Rose Richards. Tina also knew she was in town and was trying to track her down herself, hoping to get her on her show as a guest. When I told her what I planned, she said she'd get right on it.

I then put in a call to Gail, my producer in Chicago, and gave her the number of Vicki Krist, Tina's producer. Gail had heard of her and said she'd give her a call. With both of us working on it, we had a better chance of scoring a hit.

By noon, I got a call from Rose herself.

"Nick Scott, this is Rose Richards. I hear you're looking for me. By the way, I'm a big fan."

"Rose! Rose Richards calling me?"

"C'mon. I'm just an ordinary person."

"With the most popular morning show in America. I don't think that's ordinary. I admire you and all that you've done."

"Well, thank you, Nick," she said in modest acknowledgment, and immediately continued with, "I heard what you want to do and you can count me in. I think it's a brilliant idea and one that needs to be addressed."

"How long are you here?"

"Another week, but if it's a scheduling problem, I'm sure I can make it work."

I thanked her and told her I'd get back to her as soon as I got some feedback from Tina and her producer. I wanted to do it as soon as possible. Now that we had Jojo and Patti working on the profiles, the more information we could put together, the better our chances of finding the killer.

I filled Norm in and then gave Raphael a call.

"I just talked to Rose Richards and she's willing to cohost a show about the recent suicides. Isn't that great?"

"Sounds somewhat depressing," he said.

"Why do I get the feeling you don't want me to pursue this? You hired us as consultants and we seem to be making some headway, but every time I tell you about it, you discourage it. You want us to stop working the case?"

"No, not at all. It's just that I'm getting some heat about it."

"From who?"

"Can't talk about it now. Will you be around this evening?"

"Should be. I can make time for you."

"That would be nice. How about meeting me for dinner around six and we can talk more about it."

"Sounds great."

"I'll pick you up around five thirty."

"Sounds good."

I started thinking about the show and how exciting it would be to cohost with Rose. After all she had been through, she was my hero and now that she had come out, she was a role model for many gay people everywhere. I wondered if she'd consider being a guest on my show back in Chicago. I'd ask her in person, once we finished the show here.

Just then the phone rang. It was Tina.

Before we even said hello, she launched an attack. "You could have let me try to get Rose on my own, Nick. You didn't have to get the producers involved. It made me look useless."

Another case of a bruised ego. Our business was filled with prima donnas who constantly wanted their egos stroked.

"Sorry, Tina. I was just trying to get the job done. The more people on it, the better our chances of landing Rose, and look, it worked. I'm sorry if I overstepped."

"I didn't mean to snap at you. You're right. This isn't about me, but I wanted to be the one who got the credit."

"Tina, I know how it works. Everyone wants to get a notch on his belt. How long have you been doing this now?"

"Two years."

"I'm new at this, too. I'm not trying to be patronizing, but you know we're in a competitive business. One could even say cut-throat. I've learned that you get farther by working together, rather than doing it all yourself. People remember favors, especially the higher you get. They'll remember your cooperation and willingness to make them look good, and that makes you look better."

I knew I was dealing with someone who felt she would be cut out of the loop at any moment. The truth is, it did happen, but there were also good people in the business.

I continued. "I'm grateful for what you did on the first show and for what you're doing now. This could be crucial in catching the killer. Won't you be proud to be part of that if it happens?"

"Definitely."

"Okay. Have you come up with a slot when we could do this? Rose, Norm, and I are on board as your cohosts for the show, and if we could give Rose some idea of scheduling, I know she'd appreciate it. She's on vacation, too."

"There's a possibility for tomorrow afternoon. I have to clear it with technical because of the call-in feature. I'll let you know as soon as I know."

"Thanks, Tina. You're really going to be famous one day. Mark my words."

33

DINNER WITH RAPHAEL

By the end of the day, everyone was finally on board for a four o'clock show the next afternoon. Tina would serve as moderator, while Rose, Norm, and I would cohost. It would be an hour show, half an hour devoted to Tina asking us questions and then the other half devoted to listeners calling in. Promos were already going out saying that Rose Richards would join Norm and me for a special on the recent suicides, especially involving Moss, Knowles, Baxter, and Turino. Anyone who knew them well or had something to say would be encouraged to call during the last half hour of the show.

Now that the show was set, I felt we were getting someplace. Norm was pleased, and Patti had been working on the profiles and would have something to present to us this evening.

I told them I had dinner plans but would be home by nine o'clock at the latest, so we could go over her findings.

Raphael picked me up at five thirty and we headed to Martin's, a German restaurant on Duval.

"You'll like this place. Good food, good people."

"You go there often?" I asked.

"Only on special occasions."

"Is this a special occasion?"

"Anytime I'm with you is a special occasion."

"Flattery will get you everywhere."

"That's what I was hoping for."

I filled him in on my mother's departure and what happened between Norm and her.

"I like your mom. She's a real character."

"That's for sure. She can be overbearing at times."

"But that's because you're her son. How's Norm holding up?" Raphael asked.

"Fine. Like nothing happened." I decided it was time to learn more about Raphael. I knew very little about his personal life.

"What about your mom? You never talk about her."

"She died when I was young. I was only ten. What I remember of her I treasure. She was tender and loving and laughed a lot. After she died, my older sister and Papi took care of me. A few years later, he remarried. He was always busy, but since I was the youngest and a boy, everyone spoiled me, even my stepmother."

"Rotten, I'd say."

"You could say that but there could be repercussions."

"Maybe you've noticed I say what's on my mind."

"I've noticed."

We were driving in his convertible and it was a beautiful night. I enjoyed the wind in my hair and my face and being next to him. All of it was starting to feel right. We were still in the honeymoon stage and enjoying it. I wanted it to stay that way forever. When we got to the restaurant, Raphael and I got out and he waved for the valet. *Spoiled* didn't even come close to describing him. *Entitled* seemed to be a better fit.

Martin's had open-air tables overlooking Duval, and the atmosphere was classy without being stuffy: white tablecloths, black-tie waiters, and warm Florida shrimp as appetizers.

We each had a dirty martini made to perfection. Raphael recommended the pistachio-crusted yellowtail snapper, homemade German potato salad, and asparagus tips. He planned to have a filet mignon, the restaurant's special orzo, mixed with tomatoes, onion, and feta, and a small arugula salad.

As we waited for our orders, I said, "You mentioned you were getting some heat. What's that about?"

"I don't know if I told you or not but my dad used to be chief of police here, and the Bubbas are used to things running a certain way."

"What way is that?" I asked, curious.

"Not to bring attention to anything unpleasant."

"Even if it might be a murder?"

"That's just it. Key West doesn't have murders. We are a tourist town where everything runs smoothly. Everyone comes here for sun and fun."

"But, Raphael, something else is going on here."

"I know what you're saying but it's causing waves."

"With people other than the Bubbas?"

Our meals arrived and Raphael stopped the conversation. He wanted to keep this private.

We ate in silence. The fish was tender and flaky and the potato salad was served warm. It was an excellent meal, but then, I hadn't eaten a bad one yet.

I begged off on wine with dinner because I knew if I drank more, I wouldn't be going back to my house. It would be another night at the guesthouse, and as much as I wanted to be with Raphael, I also wanted to work on the cases. Being properly prepared for the show was essential.

"As you were saying."

"Bubbas run this town. I'm sure you've heard that. They hold a lot of power. If they want something, they get it, and if they don't, there's hell to pay."

I was beginning to feel uncomfortable. Raphael had been given a warning, and it was one that seemed to be in conflict with everything I believed a good cop should be.

"Go on."

"I've been asked to have you withdraw from the TV show with Rose. In other words, don't do it."

I felt my mouth drop open a slight bit and looked at him like I was seeing a stranger. This was a guy I had slept with, someone I shared confidences with about my family and myself. I couldn't believe he was asking me to do this. The honeymoon was over, and the relationship might be next.

"What happens if I refuse?" I asked.

"I won't be able to guarantee your safety. I'd suggest you return to Chicago."

"Or what?"

He looked down at his plate, refused to look me in the eyes, and didn't answer the question. He was pleading silence.

"What about us?" I asked.

"That's why I'm begging you to stop the show. I've never felt this way about anyone. I mean it, and I'd like you to stick around."

"You'll need to be a bit clearer on that."

"I like you, Nick. I think I might even love you, and I'd like to see where we go from here."

I had begun to have similar feelings and I wanted to see how our relationship would develop, too. But now that I heard he wanted me to back down because of some threats from the Bubbas, I began to lose respect for him.

"Who asked you to do this?"

"I already told you."

"I think there's more to this than you're telling me."

"The less you know at this point, the better."

I couldn't let this slide. "Did your father ask that I drop the show?"

He played with the edge of the napkin, then moved to the silverware, tapping the knife against the table. "Yes."

"Do you think it's the right thing to do?" I asked him.

"This doesn't have anything to do with the right thing. You know that from working as a cop. Often the wrong thing becomes the right thing to do, depending on who's doing it."

"But this is serious, Raphael. If these people were murdered, there is a huge cover-up going on, and you're going to be part of it."

"I beg you not to go through with it. There's a lot more involved here than you think."

I pushed my plate away, stood up, and pushed my chair back into its place.

"I'd like to go back now. I am going to do the show and I refuse to be threatened by you, the Bubbas, or your father. Guests lost their lives for appearing on my show even though I warned them of the consequences. They insisted on coming on even if it meant their death because they believed in principles. Principles matter, Raphael. We're able to sit here and have dinner and talk openly about our feelings for each other because we stand on the shoulders of those who went before us. Don't you get that?"

"Please don't do this, Nick."

"What? You want me to go back to the guesthouse with you so you can convince me? I wonder if any of your actions have been real. Maybe you're used to getting anyone you want, and as long as you're a good boy and listen to Daddy, everything is fine."

"Nick, stop, please."

"It's time you listened to the truth. I'm a cop, a cop who believes in doing the right thing, even if it means losing my job or my life. That's why I signed up. I nearly lost my life not too long ago, and it was to put away a killer."

"Can you keep it down, please?"

"You're lucky I'm not screaming even louder. I am doing the show," I said, loud enough for the other customers to stop and look at us. "Norm and I will get to the bottom of this. I don't know why you hired us as consultants unless it was just another one of your ploys to have sex with me."

"I'll take you home."

"Never mind. I'd rather walk."

"I'm going to be in trouble with a lot of people."

"That's your problem. Grow some balls and do the right thing."

With that, I left him at the table and took off. I clenched my teeth. My meal wasn't sitting well. I needed to get back to see what Patti had uncovered.

Raphael and I had just fallen out of paradise and gone straight into the battle trenches of hell.

34

Everyone was surprised to see me back by eight.

"What happened?" Norm asked.

"Raphael asked me not to do the show."

"He what?"

"His dad and the Bubbas don't want us to stir the pot. Everything is fine as long as they control everything. We're making them nervous."

"That means there's a lot more going on here than we think."

"You got it."

"Patti worked on these profiles for a long time and came up with some interesting findings."

"I want to hear all about it."

Patti was in the pool with the boys, even though it was late. It was still warm and, like most young kids, they couldn't get enough of being in the water. They could be shivering and blue, but they would continue to play as long as they could.

Norm showed me Patti's notes, and she was a skilled professional. None of the suicides fit the standard profile for depression. None had means, motive, or previous attempts. None had any psychiatric history or serious problems. In other words, they had no reason to kill themselves. Patti left a sticky note on top of the pile. "Need to talk when you have a minute."

It usually took time to collect the information for psych evals, and the best way to do that was to interview the person, but of course they were all dead. Patti worked nonstop. She depended on public records and any information she could gather from relatives or current friends, which was difficult, since they were still grieving. The fact that little of this information had made it into the case files only made me more suspicious.

After going over the files and making some notes for the show, I decided I needed to unwind. I got on one of the house bikes and told the gang I was going for a ride. I wasn't in the mood to talk to Patti about the cases yet.

I threw on a tank top and a pair of shorts, got on a mountain bike, and sped off. I took Atlantic Boulevard and made my way to the ocean. It was still warm. I felt the wind behind my back and heard the waves hitting the shore.

I must have pedaled for thirty minutes before I noticed I was being followed. A black SUV was letting other cars pass it, keeping me in sight. I knew a tail when I saw one and decided this could be dangerous. The show was tomorrow and I already knew people didn't want me to do it.

I sped up and tried to get ahead of the SUV to make sure I was right. The driver tried to stay a couple of car lengths away, but when I got farther than that, the car sped up. I had lost tails before and knew I had to get off the main drag.

I tried another surge, and when I saw my chance, I cut in front of oncoming cars, hearing some of them screech to a stop to avoid hitting me, and made it to the other side. I headed for the cover of the mangroves that had a few trails into the heart of darkness. I figured I could either get lost in the underbrush or leave the bike behind and make my way back home on foot.

I found a well-traveled bike path and took it, not knowing where it would lead me. At least I wouldn't be an open target.

When the path became too hard to see, I ditched the bike. I stayed in the shadows as I tried to make my way back. The car had turned around, and I saw the arc of a searchlight trying to find me in the brush. I stayed low.

Then I saw a group of Harley bikers coming up the boulevard. They had seen the car's occupants using the spotlight and decided to slow them down for the fun of it. They rode as a group of sixteen, blocking anyone from getting around them. I had to smile at their sense of rebellion. They had given me time to make some headway.

One of them saw me trying to escape, slowed down, and said, "You need a lift?"

"Oh yeah, brother."

"Hop on."

As soon as I was in place, he sped up toward the front of the group, letting the leader know he had picked up a passenger. They must have had their own secret language, because the head honcho nodded and they made another formation, where some stayed in front of the SUV, others surrounded it, and a few fell in behind it so the car couldn't go more than five miles an hour. The group formation could have passed as a presidential patrol, except these escorts were bikers with beards, jean jackets, and red scarves.

"Where you need to go?" my biker asked.

I gave him directions. He nodded and turned to his group and wound up his finger, meaning, "Let's wrap this up."

Four of the bikers pulled out 9-mm pistols and shot out the tires of the SUV, causing it to swerve and come to a complete halt. Then they sped up to keep pace with the group, leaving the occupants of the SUV to jump out, waving their guns in the air, swearing at the bikers. I wondered if it was in English, Spanish, or Russian.

Five minutes later, I was back at the ranch, thinking of my dangerous brush with death and grateful for the renegade group of ragtag outlaws that had just saved my life.

Once I told Norm what happened, he said, "It's not safe for Patti and the boys to stay here any longer. I'm going to ask Brooks to be here twenty-four-seven for their protection. Patti found out some crucial information. When she spoke to Mrs. Moss, Tom's wife, Mrs. Moss confirmed that Tom never would have used *a-holes* in any kind of note, especially a suicide note. When he was angry, he often used the word *assholes*. She tried to tell the police and they said they'd look into it. So far, no one has."

"More proof he may have been coerced and it was a murder. Patti and the boys have to leave here tomorrow."

35

We were at the TV station by three thirty. We did the meet-
and-greet with Rose Richards, and she was as gracious and beautiful as she was on her show. She was wearing a tight-fitting magenta
silk dress and a smile that lit up the room.

I filled her in on what we had found and, being a 24/7 professional, she said, "This is going to be good. Let's show them what
we've got."

Since this was a special event for Key West, the show had been
moved to the Tennessee Williams Theater at Lower Keys Community College, the largest venue on the island. Cameras had already
been put in place, sound equipment checked, and the set config-
ured to accommodate callers. The theater was generally used for
the finer events that came to the island, such as one-night shows by
marquee talent like Ben Vereen or the New York City Ballet.

As showtime approached, I was surprised to see that the theater was packed to its seating capacity of two hundred. Word spread
quickly and tickets went fast for something worth seeing. Rose suggested the proceeds be used to start a Keys suicide hotline along
with a Lifeline drop-in center for groups, a brilliant idea and much

needed in the community. Many volunteers had already offered their services.

Vicki stood to the right side of the camera, ready to do the countdown to the show.

Five seconds to air. I was surprised to see Raphael sitting in the front row. Had he been told to show up to intimidate me, or was he there to be supportive? I felt sad that I had begun to mistrust him. Everything had seemed to be going so well. Then I wondered if his father had been behind last night's attempt to tail me or maybe even kill me. Even worse—what if Raphael himself was behind it? Maybe it was a ritual to prove he could hold his own with the gang of Bubbas. Norm would probably say I was going through one of my conspiracy theories and being paranoid, but still.

The stage was set up similar to that of a political debate broadcast. Tina sat on a platform about a foot higher than the stage, much like a political moderator, while Rose sat in the middle of a semicircle onstage, flanked on each side by Norm and me. Cameras were set up to focus on Tina or us, and to take a wide shot, which included all of us.

Three, two, one. We were on air.

"Welcome to our our special broadcast. I'm Tina Stafford, and I'm happy to introduce my three special cohosts today: Rose Richards, host of *America Today*; Nick Scott, host of *The Gay Detective*; and his partner, Detective Norm Malone. Our topic today is suicides in the Keys. As you know, within the last year, the number of suicides has doubled, and although we touched on the subject in a recent show, our cohosts are here to discuss a few of the specifics that have recently been uncovered regarding Commissioner Tom Moss, Senator Sean Baxter, DEA officer Patrick Knowles, and police officer Junior Turino. As to format, I may be asking each of my cohorts specific questions, but they will also be talking directly to each other. Later, we will have call-ins from our viewers. Let's begin. Rose?"

ROSE: "Thank you, Tina. It is my pleasure to be here today. Key West is one of my favorite getaways and one of the most relaxing and beautiful cities in the country. When I was contacted about taking part in this special, I accepted gladly, since, first, I am saddened that anyone would want to take their life."

TINA: "Nick has hosted *The Gay Detective* for over a year now, and he and his partner, Norm Malone, were responsible for tracking down the serial killer The Reaper. Nick, do you have any new information to share with us about these victims?"

NICK: "First, let me say it is an honor to be cohosting this show with Rose, and I am pleased to be part of this panel. Norm and I were asked to be consultants on the cases since the chief felt we could lend some of our expertise as detectives from Chicago, where the number of suicides is much higher. From the start, we thought that Commissioner Moss's suicide was unusual because he had no reason to take his own life."

TINA: "Have any facts surfaced that would rule out suicide?"

NORM: "Let me say I've worked as a Chicago detective for over twenty years and the answer is no. But information has surfaced that makes the deaths look suspicious. I was appalled when I learned that the suicides may in fact have been murders. We have been working closely with Chief Perez, and we all want to get to the bottom of this, but as you know yourself, Rose, things move slower here."

ROSE: "Yes, they do, which is part of the appeal for me, except when it comes to solving possibly mysterious deaths."

NORM: "We have had briefings with a medical examiner and recently had a psychologist work up some profiles on the subjects."

ROSE: "Were any of the victims experiencing any major life stressors such as loss of a job, divorce, a move, illness, or death of a loved one?"

NICK: "Not one of them was going through anything like that. As you know, we all get depressed from time to time and have challenges we think are insurmountable, but with time, support, medication, and a therapist, or some combination of those treatments, depression can be treated."

ROSE: "There's also the stigma associated with depression, though awareness and education have been making inroads in decreasing that stigma. Therapy and medication do work, people. It takes a strong person to admit he needs help. On a personal note, when I was diagnosed with cancer, I wasn't sure I would make it. There were many times I thought of throwing in the towel, but the support and prayers I got from friends and fans was so amazing, I felt I couldn't disappoint them. I now have a special appreciation for the life God has given me."

NICK: "Since you're sharing… I know when my partner of fifteen years, Darren, was murdered last year, I never thought I would get through it, either. I have to admit I thought of ending it all at times, but the department ordered I see a therapist if I wanted to come back to work. Not everyone can afford a therapist, but there are clinics out there that operate on a sliding scale. Also, in many of the major cities, there is a suicide hotline that has proved to be very helpful for those who need immediate help."

ROSE: "And, hopefully, there will be one beginning in the Keys in the near future as a result of the proceeds from the tickets of today's show."

There was a large round of applause from the audience.

NORM: "Hotlines help but so do groups. I joined a survivors' group after I lost my wife to cancer. I was depressed and the group helped me. At first I was shy about sharing, but now I look forward to being part of it. It helps to share or to offer support."

TINA: "We need to stop on that positive note for a message from our sponsors, but we'll be right back."

During the break, Rose leaned in and said to me, "We need to get to the murders without blasting the police department for possible cover-ups."

"I know. I'll take your lead," I said.

Rose laughed. "I was going to take yours."

"Because I'm a detective?"

"Because you're the Gay Detective and you outrank me."

I smiled and nodded. "Jump in anytime. We do need to get to the personals on these victims."

"I've got your back," Rose said.

"What am I? Chopped liver?" Norm chimed in.

"You're better. You're my partner and you always have me covered, except when you're a jerk, of course."

Norm pretended he was offended and then slammed his fist into his open hand, imitating Jackie Gleason's "One of these days, Alice" gesture.

Rose laughed. "You guys are hysterical. You should take your act on the road."

"We are," Norm said, and laughed along.

It was a delight to work with Rose, who was so competent and easygoing. She was determined that these lives would not be lost in vain, and she was doing everything for the cause.

Vicki gave us the signal that we were back on air.

NICK: "As we were saying before the break, the victims did not have the normal stressors that are often associated with suicides. In other words, they all seemed to be well-adjusted average citizens involved in stressful jobs, but ones they chose and loved."

ROSE: "Is there any reason you can see, as a detective, why these cases were classified as suicides rather than murders?"

NICK: "Great question, Rose. Norm and I have been wondering about that ourselves. We have been having ongoing discussions with the chief and the officers involved. We hope to find some answers soon."

I could see Raphael glaring at me from the audience. Without saying it directly, I was suggesting there had been a cover-up. I'm sure it was not the answer he was hoping to hear.

TINA: "You have all made important points and given us food for thought. We need to stop here for another break, but when we come back, we'll be taking questions from callers. The number is 800-555-0000. The number again is 800-555-0000. Our callers will be able to ask or discuss any of these issues with our guests."

I took a deep breath while we were off-air. Our audience was very talkative, and it was obvious our show was creating a buzz. When we went live again, though, everybody quieted quickly for the first call.

TINA: "Caller, you're on the air."

CALLER ONE: "My name is Bob and I was a close friend of Patrick's. I want to say that I saw Patrick two days before the so-called suicide. Patrick was in good spirits and we even made plans to go see the Swayzes at the Parrot that weekend."

NICK: "Bob, thanks for calling in. How long did you know Patrick?"

BOB: "We knew each other since high school. Patrick was one of the most compassionate people I knew. And he loved to have a good time. We went to many parties, sailed together, and often drank too much."

ROSE: "From your experience with Patrick, did you ever get any hints he was depressed or did he ever mention suicide to you?"

BOB: "Never. Patrick was one of those people who didn't dwell on problems. He might get angry or sad once in a while like we all do, but after ten minutes, he let it go."

ROSE: "Thank you for calling in, Bob. I'm sorry for your loss."

BOB: "Thank you."

TINA: "Our producer is indicating that our callboard is completely lit up, so please be patient. We will try to get to as many of you as possible. Next caller, you're on the air."

CALLER TWO: "This call is for Norm."

NORM: "Yeah."

CALLER TWO: "My name is Fred. You and your partner are detectives from Chicago, and you come down here and think you can solve our cases when you don't even know our people. Who do you think you are? If anyone knows what they're doing, it's Chief Perez and his officers."

NORM: "Fred, Chief Perez is a good man and I agree with you about us being strangers to your island. But we didn't come down here to work on any cases. We came here for a vacation and were asked to help out by Chief Perez."

FRED: "So stop meddling and go back to Chicago or wherever you're from, with that sissy you're working with."

There was an audible click.

ROSE: "I hope Fred doesn't belong to any welcoming committees. His use of derogatory terms is not only rude, it's unbecoming from someone who knows the motto here is One Human Family."

CALLER THREE: "Hello. I'm Andrea Baxter, the wife of the late Congressman Sean Baxter." She held back a sob and took a moment before continuing. "Please bear with me. This is so difficult."

ROSE: "Take your time. I'm sure this must be very painful for you."

ANDREA: "Thank you. I was married to Sean for twelve years and he was one of the most caring, loving husbands and fathers you could ever meet. In fact, he was thinking of making a presidential bid in 2020. I'm calling to say that there is no way Sean would have taken his own life. He was happy and made everyone around him feel the same."

ROSE: "I appreciate your sharing that. There's no way I can know what you're going through, but please believe me when I say our thoughts and prayers are with you."

ANDREA: "Thank you, Rose. That means a lot to me."

CALLER FOUR: "Hi, my name is Lorie. I was a friend of Junior's. I met him at Bobbi's Monkey Bar. Everyone there loved him. He'd drop in for a drink and that's how we got to know each other. Occasionally, he'd come in the evenings for karaoke. There's no way he would kill himself. We talked about taking a trip to Italy one day."

NICK: "Really?"

LORIE: "Yeah, we both wanted to go to Venice and ride a gondola together."

ROSE: "So the two of you were close."

LORIE: "We had fringe benefits, as the kids say, but he shied away from a commitment.

NICK: "Did he ever seem depressed to you?"

LORIE: "He'd feel down sometimes, like we all do, but I'd buy him a drink or someone else would and before you knew it, he'd laugh it off. The next day he'd be fine."

ROSE: "Had he ever talked about Congressman Baxter, Commissioner Moss, or Patrick Knowles to you?"

LORIE: "Not that I can remember."

NICK: "Thanks for your call."

CALLER FIVE: "My name is Sarah and I'm Tom Moss's daughter. I just want to say my dad wasn't around a lot because of his work, but when he was, he tried to be a good dad. I loved him a lot and will miss him."

NORM: "How old are you, Sarah?"

SARAH: "Fifteen."

ROSE: "How was your dad right before he died?"

SARAH: "He seemed fine. Busy but fine. We talked about going sailing the next day."

ROSE: "I'm sorry for your loss, Sarah. Nothing can take away all the memories you had with your dad. Try to remember those."

SARAH: "Thank you, Rose. I appreciate that."

NICK: "I'd like to add that, as many of you heard, their loved ones seemed normal, not depressed. In some suicides individuals are elated right before they kill themselves. It's because they have made a plan and decided to follow through with it. That being said, from what I've heard so far, it doesn't sound like these possible suicides had such a plan in place."

ROSE: "Then what should friends or family be looking for?"

NORM: "Previous attempts, giving away money or prized possessions, insomnia, over- or under eating, asking if you'd take care of their pet if something happened to them are some things I've heard are glaring giveaways."

The hour had slipped away and Tina interrupted the Q and A.

TINA: "I'm afraid we've run out of time. I want to thank Rose, Nick, and Norm for being cohosts on our show, and a special thanks to our listeners for calling in today. Are there any last words from our hosts?"

ROSE: "I want to thank you, Tina, for having me on; my cohosts; and all of the callers who so openly shared their feelings with us. I know how difficult it is to lose someone, and we heard what those losses have meant to family, lovers, and friends. My heart and prayers go out to my special One Human Family."

NICK: "I want to make a point of how important this has been to me. As a detective, I see a lot of death, and it's never pleasant. We often don't hear about the pain that is left behind. We are here to help and in no way to criticize the work that is being done by the Key West Police Department."

NORM: "Nick's right. Our best work is when the community joins us so that we all work together. If there is a murderer out there, help us catch the bastard."

TINA: "Thanks again to our panel and to the callers for making this show so special. If you have information you think can be helpful, please call us at 800-555-0000 or call the Key West police directly. I am Tina Stafford, wishing you a pleasant evening."

Afterward, I was able to talk to Rose for a short time and she invited me to come on her show and I reciprocated. I was sorry that we had to meet under such circumstances, but we couldn't control that. What we did control was what we could do.

Right now, I knew Norm and I were on the same page. We were sure someone had murdered the last four victims. What we had to find out was why. I didn't think I was going to get much help from Raphael. In fact, I wasn't sure I'd be seeing him again. He had already left the theater and hadn't left me any messages.

36

SHARK ATTACK

When Norm and I got back to the house, Patti was sitting at the pool as the boys played in the water. Nathan was snoring loudly under Patti's chair, showing just how excited he was to see us. Officer Brooks had stationed himself a few feet away and gave us a nod.

"Hey, guys. I listened to the show. You were great. Both of you," Patti said.

"You'd say anything to stay a few more days," Norm said.

"*Daad.*"

The boys noticed we were back and waved to us. They were using foam noodles to stay afloat but kept falling off.

"C'mon in and play with us," Johnny said.

I got a text from Jojo.

> Need to meet. Important.

I showed the text to Norm.

"We'll be back soon," I said.

"Promise?" Mark said.

"Promise," Norm said. "And then we'll play Shark Attack."

"Yes, Shark Attack," I said, using my hands to look like jaws.

"Yay!" they shouted back.

We met Jojo at the end of the AIDS Memorial located at the entrance to White Street Pier. The names of AIDS victims were etched on black memorial plaques set into the sides of the pier, dotted with benches and lit by colonial-style lights. Often the surf was so high it drenched unsuspecting tourists, who liked to walk or bike on the pier. The memorial provided a stunning view of the shore, the jetty, and the sunset.

We walked and talked quietly, the only potential witnesses privy to our conversation long departed, having lost their battle with AIDS.

Jojo began, "I've finished the follow-up on the 801 girls and their whereabouts after the accident. They've all been accounted for. Most went back to the club for a two a.m. show. The only ones who were suspicious were Ora and Mimi. Ora claimed nausea and went home, and Mimi was late for her show by twenty minutes. Something she never does."

"We need to look into that," Norm said.

"When I left the police station, I thought about the victims," Jojo continued. "Two were in politics and two were with law enforcement. Somehow they had to be linked. Politicians and the police have worked together in illegal activities before. A contractor could be set up to handle all the dirty business: visas, working papers, and jobs, while illegals could be brought in to do the actual drug deliveries."

"They get here with the promise of the American Dream, only to find they are indentured servants. It's a form of human trafficking in an intricate web." Norm added.

"Maybe that's why so many Slavs work here," I said.

"It's ingenious, actually," Jojo continued. "The dealers subcontract to the trafficked workers: taxi drivers, hotel staff, bartenders, and dancers, to name a few, who must then give a third of their wages to the dealers in return for a work visa. Now that they have local blue-collar workers, they then start to solicit city, county, and federal agencies, looking for one black sheep in each division willing to get dirty and make extra money. They could use UPS drivers, mailmen, DEA officers, anyone who is willing to stay in his job while dealing."

"It's a clever strategy. If a dealer received a shipment and had a mailing list of buyers, he had several ways of sending it. The seller could package it and have the post office deliver it to a specific address," I said.

"The dealer could have an in-house person at the post office to make sure the packages got through, and a specific mailman to deliver," I continued.

Norm shook his head. "The system, with minimal variations, could also be applied to the staff in the service industries, such as bars, hotels, and B and Bs."

Jojo continued with his thoughts and the results of his investigation. "I searched the phone records of the last four suicides and found a number that repeated itself. I got a trace on it and it belonged to the administrative offices of an export-import business."

He explained, "I tried to get an appointment with the chairman of the board but found out he had died recently. No one was being cooperative, so I ran it by Milo. It so happens the chairman of the board was none other than Tom Moss. Then it hit me. Each of the victims had stock in the business. With more digging, I found their aliases, and each one was on the board."

"So each of them was dealing drugs for the cartel?" I asked.

"Whoa," Jojo said. "That doesn't prove they were dealing drugs. It means they were all partners in a well-known company. Leaders don't want to get dirty. They invest."

"Not surprising for Moss, but the other three don't seem to fit the profile," Norm said.

"Unless they were being blackmailed," Jojo said. "We know Moss had a secret male lover. He owned a lot of businesses, so where'd he get the money?"

"That works. He could have also been laundering the cash through his other businesses," I said.

"But Patrick, Sean, and Junior? How do they fit?" Norm asked.

"Sean Baxter was a congressman. He needed campaign money to get elected. What if he received finances in exchange for over-looking search restrictions? Super PACs are opaque entities with millions of dollars to be used toward a candidate's benefit.

"Possible, but no evidence," Jojo reminded us. "I also had a chat with his wife. I wrote down some notes after the interview.

Andrea Baxter was afraid her husband was hanging out with some *dirty* characters and was frightened for her family and his planned presidential campaign. Sean told her to mind her own business. He also added that if anything happened to him she should move somewhere obscure, like South America. This fright-ened and angered her because they had always worked as a close, loving couple.

"So Sean might have been on the take, might even have planned to run for president of the United States," Norm said.

"And if he tried to get out, something would happen to him or his family, or maybe he could be exposed. Leaks happen all the time in politics, and accusations turn into perceived or alternative facts and spread faster than wild fire," I added.

"He tried to get out and ended up dead. The killer made it look like a suicide."

"Bingo," Norm said.

"So we have one potential blackmail and one I-won't-play-anymore," I said.

"Knowles and Turino were both law enforcement, one federal and one local," Jojo said. "Turino was undercover, so he may have been protecting one of the cartel members, who supervised drops, or he may have been arranging deals himself. Either way, he was in the perfect position to act as an intermediary."

"So why kill him?"

"I got a trace on Turino's accounts. He had one million spread over two banks here and had offshore accounts in the Caymans."

"Skimming?" I asked.

"Most likely. Once the cartel discovered it, Junior was toast. Another assisted suicide."

"And Knowles?"

"I talked to his lover, Bob. He called in today, remember? Nothing that will stand up under scrutiny, but I'll bet my Merlot that Knowles was being threatened to stay in line or something could happen to Bob."

"Still doesn't tell us who it was," I said.

"The cartel has links all over the Cuban community. Everyone is afraid to say anything about them because they've got power and clout," Jojo said.

"Well, that explains the Cuban influence, but what about the Slavic one?" I asked.

"They may have been working together or parallel, each making sure not to step on the other's toes," Norm said. "Drug cartel works import and trafficking does distribution. Perfect setup."

"Makes me think Raphael knows a lot more than he's letting on. Also explains why he's been so casual about the suicides, asking me to stop digging so much. It explains a lot of things."

Raphael had used me. He asked us to be consultants just as a ruse to get me into bed. Why was I so naive? I was vulnerable, but I was also stupid. I should have seen that. *None of this would have happened if Darren were still alive,* I thought.

I felt bile rise in my throat. Then I remembered he hadn't left by choice, as my shrink often pointed out. My anger and sadness were triggered by survivor's guilt.

Norm knew what I was thinking.

"Both of us fell for the consultant gig, Nick. Let's face it. We both like solving crimes. That's not a bad thing. You couldn't have known," Norm said, trying to ease my pain.

I gave a small grin in appreciation and would have thanked him if I hadn't been so angry with myself.

I'd been had in more ways than one.

37

Norm hadn't slept well worrying about Patti and the two
boys. He was glad they were returning to Chicago today.

The cops were watching everything we did, and we already
knew someone had been tailing me very aggressively, trying to run
me off the road, maybe even kill me.

I strongly agreed with his decision since I'd never forgive myself
if something happened to any of them.

"Can we take Nathan with us?" Mark asked.

I looked at Norm, wondering what he'd say, since it was an awkward question. Nathan might be happier with the boys, but none of
us anticipated this. We didn't know if Patti was on board for having a dog. She had her hands full as it was. We hadn't given much
thought to Nathan's future. He had become part of the family and
we assumed he'd stay with us. I decided it was Norm's call. I'd go
along with whatever he decided.

"He was given to me as a gift, Mark. Otherwise, I'd say yes, but
you're welcome to come play with him anytime and maybe he can
do sleepovers with you. How's that?"

"When are you coming back?" Johnny asked.

"Today's Wednesday. We'll probably be back home by Sunday. That's not far away."

"Okay," Johnny said, knowing it wouldn't be long.

They both gave us hugs, and Nathan gave them kisses. They had all bonded in a very short time. Nathan wasn't a watchdog, but he'd kill you with kindness if you let him.

We drove them to the airport, which was only ten minutes away, and saw them off.

"Thank you for looking out for us, Dad," Patti said. "Please be careful."

"We will, but we need to follow this through."

"I understand." She paused. "Thanks, guys. We enjoyed our vacation. Mike said they're predicting a blizzard by tomorrow. I'll keep a picture of us by the pool on the kitchen table until summer."

———

NOW WE COULD GET BACK to the case without worrying about Patti and the kids.

Jojo had given us a lot of information. The problem was, we couldn't trust the chief with it. All our ducks, or chickens in this case, were wandering around aimlessly, nowhere close to being in a row. We might even need to call in the FBI, since we didn't know how far the frame had gone. Norm thought of informing the DA, but she had decided to retire at the end of this term and was currently on vacation.

———

THAT EVENING I got an anonymous text:

> Go back to Chicago.
> NOW.

There was no way to trace it. It was an attempt to keep us off the case. We were getting close. Now that the callers had provided the truth, the police were getting some heat from the community. The text could have been from anyone, but I would have guessed it was from Raphael.

Jojo had told us he was meeting with Milo that evening and was then going to see Merlot. We didn't expect him to come back home.

He called us an hour later.

"Meet me at the Red Carter as soon as you can." It was now midnight.

"What's up?" I asked.

"Need to talk in person. ASAP."

38

After the show, Jojo had met up with Merlot. She only had
two more nights to her run, and Jojo had been to every one of her
shows.

When we got to the Red Garter, he was waiting outside the
door, looking distressed.

"Nick, you're in danger."

We left Duval and decided to go to White Street Pier. At that
time, there wouldn't be anyone else there, and we could talk in
private.

Jojo, able to weave through traffic on his scooter, was waiting
for us at the edge of the pier. He motioned for us to join him.

It was still in the eighties, and the humidity had started to
climb. A storm was predicted. The winds were coming in at fifteen
miles per hour, causing the waves to hit the walls and splash surf
another five feet higher. We had to walk in the middle of the pier
to avoid getting wet.

He didn't waste any time telling us what happened.

"Yesterday, Milo sold an unmarked .22 caliber pistol to a guy
named Tony, whom he knows to be a hitman for the cartel. He told

Merlot about it in casual conversation and pointed Tony out to her at the show. Milo and I are tight now, so he doesn't want any one of us to get hurt."

Jojo continued. "Tony was gaga over Merlot last night, so she took him home with her and slipped him something. He was already half-loaded, and it didn't take long for him to start blabbing. Merlot said she was afraid he'd go out before she got any dirt, but she's good. She could even work for us, if we wanted."

"What did she say?" I asked. I decided not to pursue her future as an undercover agent.

"Word's out about us, and the cartel doesn't like bad press. Their way of dealing with that is usually done quickly and quietly. He was told to kill you, Nick. It's their way of sending a message."

"They don't know us very well, do they?" I said.

"We've been here before. Same show, bad episode, wrong ending," Norm said.

"We need to stop Tony before anything happens to you, Nick," Jojo said.

"But there's someone giving orders to Tony. We need to find the boss behind this. Otherwise, everything goes back to usual. They find different dealers who cooperate with them. If not, they're murdered," I said.

"Did Merlot describe Tony to you?" Norm asked.

"Yeah."

The wind picked up some speed and a wave splashed over us just as Jojo was about to give us the description. We decided to get off the pier and walk along the sidewalk next to the beach. It wasn't as private, but it was almost deserted at this time of night. A police car pulled up and two cops got out of the car. One of them was

Perez. He introduced the driver as Officer Jones and then asked, "What are you guys doing out here so late?"

"Taking a stroll on the beach, Chief," Norm said.

"But there's a storm on the way."

There were many storms brewing, possibly leading to a hurricane, I thought.

"We noticed. But we're used to bad weather," I said, using Chicago belligerence. I needed to hold myself back from whipping him as badly as the wind was whipping us.

"Why don't we all get out of here and go get some coffee?" Perez suggested.

"Coffee gives me indigestion this late at night," Norm said.

"I have some Tums," Officer Jones offered. They were determined to get us off the beach and stop us from talking. I wondered if they knew what was going on or if they were fishing. It was a bad night to fish, but that didn't stop anyone who was determined. Perez was determined.

He told us to meet him and the other officer at Sandy's. We took our car and Jojo left his scooter at the pier. On the way there, Jojo quickly described Tony. We had only a few minutes before we all met up.

"He's in his thirties, six feet, two hundred twenty pounds, black beard, and a full face. Usually wears a white T-shirt with 'Havana' embossed across the front," Jojo finished up just as we pulled into the parking area.

Sandy's was open twenty-four hours, and it was 2:00 a.m. now. There were a lot more people there than I expected. A lot of the customers from the bars, most of them toasted, were ordering Cuban sandwiches and coffee. What was supposed to be a line looked like a school of fish fighting for some chum.

Officer Jones was given the job of getting the food while Raphael stayed with us to make sure nothing important was said in his absence.

As Raphael was walking to his bench, he bumped into a tall, broad-shouldered, blond Russian, and as they looked at each other, Raphael said, "Vladimir, how you been?"

"Good. Good. Nasty stuff with the suicides. What are you doing that so many are dying to get out of your jurisdiction?"

Raphael ignored his comment, apparently not wanting to get into it.

"How's Anna doing?"

"Still shook up, but getting better."

I overheard the exchange and knew the names but couldn't place them. They were familiar and I tried to pull up the memory, but it kept evading me like a dream.

"How's work?" Raphael asked.

"No complaints. The flow is constant."

"Gotta go. I've got business."

When Vladimir saw where he was staring and saw me, he said, "Nice business."

Raphael smiled.

"Be sure to say hi to Papi," Vladimir said.

"And you to Anna. We need to get together for a vodka."

"Sure thing. Call me."

"Will do."

"Nice seeing you, cuz."

The memory was almost there when Raphael approached the bench and sat down, causing it to slip away again.

Then I heard Jojo's phone ding.

He took a look at it and kept his poker face as he passed the phone to Norm and me. Merlot had sent us a pic of Tony, passed out on her couch. Jojo had given us an accurate description.

Jojo discretely swiped the screen.

"What's so interesting?" Raphael asked.

"A friend sent me a picture of a manatee."

"Let's see," Raphael demanded.

Jojo showed him.

"They're endangered," Raphael said.

"So am I," I said dryly.

Jojo rolled his tongue over his top teeth, a habit he had when he was trying to hide an expression such as a smile.

We ate in silence. After that, Raphael looked pointedly at Norm and me and said, "I want to thank you both for all your help as consultants. Your recent show has flooded our station with numerous calls. Some may be possible leads, but most were quack calls. I've been in touch with Lieutenant Brodsky."

"Um," Norm said.

"I told him what a wonderful job you guys have done and we've both agreed that you're no longer needed on the case."

Translation: Raphael was getting a lot of heat and wanted it to stop. He had even called our Chicago boss to cover his ass and thanked him for our help. Most likely, Brodsky hadn't known about our involvement and would now be happy to tell us to stop meddling in another jurisdiction's business. Not only had Raphael taken us off the case, he had also managed to get us in trouble with our boss.

"Just when we were starting to get somewhere," Norm said.

"Brodsky will be giving you a call sometime tomorrow."

"Well played," Norm said with as much sarcasm as he could.

"Thanks, guys. It's been a pleasure."

With that, Raphael got up, brushed his hands back and forth, like he had just finished cleaning up a mess, clucked his tongue, and got ready to get back into his cruiser.

Was it an act or a ruse? Either way, it was dirty. Raphael was using every technique possible to get us off the case.

Norm and I drove back to the house after we dropped Jojo by his scooter. As we pulled into our driveway, a shot rang out, nicking the front fender. We both ducked for cover. Tony hadn't wasted any time.

We saw a red scooter take off from the back of the house. We tried to pursue, but he was soon weaving in and out of traffic and we lost him.

"Think we should report it to the police?" I asked, laying on the irony.

"We're on our own now."

"You're right," I said, giving out a sigh. "How about a meter maid?"

Norm smiled.

We alerted Jojo instead.

Who knew how Tony's mind worked? He could be trigger happy or he may have received other orders. Either way, he was a loose cannon and a threat to all of us.

My memory must have been jolted. I remembered that Anna was the cleaning woman at City Hall who had found Moss's body. I had read about her in *The Citizen*. *That was the connection.*

Vladimir and Raphael were good buddies. Maybe even past lovers. It didn't prove anything other than they were close. But Vladimir knew him well enough to give his regards to Papi. If my hunch was right, they weren't just close; they were in business together. My gut told me my guess was correct. If Vladimir and his boss ran the Russian cartel and Papi and whoever ran the Cuban one, they most likely worked together and shared the spoils, agreeing not to cross boundaries.

39

We tried to come up with a strategy for our next move.

"Things are heating up. I'm glad Patti and the boys are safe."

"Me too. Now all we have to worry about is you being killed."

We both let out a bitter laugh.

As we were passing 801 on the way to the Red Garter, Ora waved us over.

Shaneeda was dressed in a low-cut silver sheath that accentuated every part of her voluptuous body. She ran and threw her arms around me and then gave Norm a huge bear hug. Surprisingly Norm hugged her back.

One huge step for Norm, I thought.

The girls once told me that their goal was to achieve acceptance, to expand thinking about gender and stereotypes. From what I just saw, they were succeeding.

Ora, who was close by and dressed in a purple wig and a black skintight evening gown, came over.

"I was waiting for you after the eleven o'clock show the other night. After the way you came on to me, I was sure we'd have some fun."

At first I didn't know what she was talking about, and then I remembered making out with her in the dressing room.

"Sorry, Ora, things got a bit complicated that night."

"Word has it you went home with the chief. I'll have to remember to wear a uniform next time, now that I know that's what you're into." She then lifted her chin up and quickly walked away from me, a scorned woman, and we all know how that one goes. But before getting out of earshot, she turned her head and said, "If there is a next time."

Norm watched the whole exchange. "What's that all about?"

"Something I don't remember well. Probably for the best."

"This may not be the time to bring this up, but I'm concerned about your blackouts. AA works well for a lot of people."

"I don't want to talk about it."

"I know you've been through a lot, but alcohol isn't the answer."

"Can we just drop this?" I said with an edge to my voice.

Eventually, we reached the Red Garter, hoping to run into Jojo. A large sign with Merlot in tails holding her dog, Gigi, was in the outdoor showcase. A banner across it said CLOSING SOON.

We entered the bar. Tony saw us. He ran.

We began the chase.

"Police! Stop!" Norm bellowed.

Tony was fast. As he ran through the hallway, he opened a couple of the doors to the private cubicles to slow us down.

I saw the back door close and ran toward it. Norm was not far behind. The customers were surprised to see an actual police chase. They didn't know what was happening, but it was as exciting as some of the stripping taking place, if not more so. Of course, there were a few customers mesmerized by Glendora's pathetic pole dance.

Tony ran at a good clip but he was never out of sight. He kept leading us farther and farther away from busy Duval Street, into Bahama Village, an area that housed a diverse population of artists and locals who were separated from the tourist mix.

Norm had fallen back, barely visible when I looked behind me. Finally, I saw Tony slip into one of the houses on Geraldine near Emma Street. Geraldine bordered the Wall, a dividing line that led back to bustling Duval. Part of the Wall was covered with graffiti by gangs and colorful figures who inhabited the village. But the Wall ended abruptly and transformed into a chain-link fence.

I hesitated going inside the house alone, knowing it was dangerous and against all protocol, but I was afraid of losing Tony. I took an aggressive stance, holding my gun in front of me, as I decided on my approach. The house was dark except for a light from a flickering streetlight, reminding me of a noir film filled with shadows and silhouettes.

Since I knew he was waiting for me to enter the front, I decided to go around and through the back. As I came around the side of the house, I heard floorboards creak inside. I tried to second-guess where he was positioning himself. The only chance I had was that of surprise.

The backyard was filled with overgrown weeds, a few cacti, and discarded toys that looked long abandoned. I had to watch that I didn't trip on the rubble.

I twisted and turned, trying to peep through the dirty windows, hoping to catch any movement inside, but it was completely dark. If I went in, I was going in blind. I would have to coordinate my entrance with the flickering streetlight. There was no pattern to the sputtering light, so I pulled out my cell, put it on flashlight, and stuck it in my belt. Putting a spotlight on my location and making myself an easy target weren't the greatest ideas, but the light at least gave me a fighting chance. I was sweating from the run and my chest heaved as I tried to catch my breath.

I ran through the door as if I were an offensive tackle, keeping my body close to the floor. A shot rang out and I felt the bullet whiz by my head, giving me a sense of where Tony was.

I slid the phone ahead of me on the floor, hoping he'd mistake the light for my location and try to shoot.

"Police. Throw your gun down and surrender!" I yelled.

Another shot rang out. My plan had worked. He aimed in the direction of the phone, and he hit it dead on. We were back in total darkness. His shot had come from the front of the house. He was checking whether Norm was going to box him in from that end, and he kept moving to make it more difficult for me to pinpoint his position.

Where the hell was Norm? He was my only backup. My luck had held out so far, but I didn't know how long it would last. I wanted to nail the bastard.

I got down on the floor and started to crawl on my elbows, soldier style, feeling it was one of the safest ways of making progress. He couldn't see me.

Norm, now standing on the front porch, said, "Drop the gun. Now."

Then another shot rang out from inside the house. Tony gave a pained groan and hit the floor like an overstuffed sack of spuds.

As I crawled a little farther, I saw Tony up close. Blood was oozing from a wound in the back of his head. He was dead. Someone else was in the house. Had this been a trap? Was it Tony's mission to bring us here for the final kill?

Then the lights went on and I was blinded by the sudden glare.

"Drop your guns. Both of you." A figure stood directly in front of us. Norm had run into the house and pushed past Tony's body. We were in the same room now.

As I looked up, I saw Dr. Mercado. He pushed his night goggles to his forehead, held a Glock, and aimed the gun at the two of us.

"Put your guns down slowly and kick them toward me. Now."

We did as instructed.

"You?" I asked in surprise.

"One and the same." He laughed maniacally.

"What are you doing here?" Norm asked.

"Stop asking questions. I give the orders. You hear me?"

"So you put out my hit?" I asked.

"Of course I did. You were starting to get too close. Tony botched the job, so I made sure I was around just in case. Drag his body in here and put him where I tell you."

We hesitated for a moment. I looked at Norm, hoping we could telepathically decide our next move. We did as he ordered, trying to delay whatever plans the doctor had, knowing they would all lead to the inevitable.

"This is going to look like there was a shootout here. Tony killed both of you, but in the process, you fatally wounded him. Tony didn't have much to lose. In fact, he was dispensable, not like the Gay Detective and his partner. What a shame."

"Were you behind the suicides, too?" I asked.

"It all makes sense now," Norm said. "You had contacts from Miami because you trained there and then you came here to distance yourself and set up a practice. You were the kingpin behind the drug cartel, making sure everyone did what you wanted. If not, you snuffed 'em."

"You're smart, Norm. Smarter than your partner. You're familiar with the streets and that's more important than any schooling. He's prettier but you're smarter. I wouldn't mind a night with you, Nick. It's unfortunate it has to end this way."

"Maybe it doesn't," I said.

"What's that supposed to mean?" Dr. Mercado said.

"Let Norm go and you can do what you want with me," I said.

The doctor laughed again. "Don't take me for a fool, Nick. You really think I'd fall for that. You're like a pretty Christmas ornament, all bling. Your offer is ridiculous."

Norm knew I was stalling. If I could distract Mercado, Norm could rush him. With no plan B, I was improvising.

"I'm really hot. I'm going to take off my shirt, Doctor."

"Don't try anything stupid, Nick," Mercado warned.

"Would you like to examine me before you kill me? After, it's not as much fun. My guess is you're kinky but not into necrophilia."

I had caught his attention. It was cheesy, I knew, but my intuition told me it was the kind of thing that would interest Mercado. So far, he hadn't told me to stop what I was doing. He was curious and hopefully distracted.

He watched me take off my shirt and throw it behind me. "That was clever what you did with the suicides. I have to give it to you. You're one of the few who could come up with such a good plan," I said.

"Thank you, Nick. I see you have a six-pack. I hope someone in the afterlife will enjoy it."

I now knew he could be distracted, distracted enough to look at my body, rather than watch our moves. *My narcissistic need for tight abs has some redeeming value after all*, I told myself.

"I'm sure you'd like to see more. How about if I slip off my pants, Doctor? Isn't that a line you use all the time? Just slip off your pants, while I examine you, maybe a prostate massage. Wouldn't you like to do that, Doctor? I'm commando, so all I need to do is take off these jeans and you'd have full nudity." I couldn't tell whether he was shocked, but I noticed a change in the intensity of his stare, and he hadn't said no.

I had been around the strippers enough to know the longer the unveiling, the more the viewer enjoyed the finale. I took my time taking off my belt and undoing my jeans, one button after another, opening a peephole of possibility for what was within. I hoped stalling would give Norm a chance to think of a distraction, since I had no idea what I'd do once I was nude. I glanced at Norm and his eyes conveyed surprise as he watched me take off my clothes.

Hoping my plan would work, I dropped my jeans, kicked them to the side, and turned so the doctor could see my profile first. In tribute to the strippers of 801, I put my hands behind my head, pulled in my glutes and slowly gave him the full monty. I would never know if that was the distraction that made Mercado lose focus, but I'm sure it didn't hurt our chances.

A brick crashed through the window and caught the doctor completely off guard. It was the moment we needed.

Norm and I rushed him, but not before Mercado fired his gun. Luckily it didn't hit anyone. Norm quickly disarmed him, while I held him down. He started to resist and I hit him squarely on the jaw, knocking him out.

Norm and I stood up, thrilled with our achievement, and high-fived each other. Not only were we celebrating capturing the doctor, we were celebrating life.

Milo had been in the Red Garter and saw us chasing Tony. He alerted Jojo, and Jojo picked Milo up at the club and they tried to follow us on the scooter but lost our trail. When they heard the shots, they drove to the house and snuck around the side until they could hear our voices.

They were too short to see through the window, so they devised a plan. They moved back as much as they could to give themselves some leverage. Jojo held out his intertwined hands, and Milo stepped into the makeshift lift and climbed onto Jojo's shoulders to create height. Jojo did his best to balance Milo as they waited for the right moment to distract the doctor. After they heard the doctor's confession, Milo threw a brick through the window.

Soon, we heard sirens, and Raphael arrived along with three other units and rushed into the house.

I looked at Raphael and he glanced at my chest and shook his head.

"Were you stripping for him?" he asked.

"Only to distract him," I said.

He shook his head and said, "Creative diversion, Nick."

We laughed as his officers cuffed the doctor and dragged him to an awaiting EMT van. Ironically, the EMT drivers were the same ones who had brought Matt into the emergency room.

40

Key West is known for its celebrations. It doesn't take much of a reason to have one, and solving four seeming suicides was big news for this town.

It was bittersweet relief for the families to learn that their loved ones, even though they were gone, had not taken their own lives. They had to accept that their significant others had somehow been involved with drugs, though, but that seemed minor. In Key West, killing was tragic news; sadly, drugs were not. As a cop, I don't approve of drugs, having seen their devastating effects.

As soon as Norm and I heard that Sho and Matt, nearly recovered, were back, we scheduled time to see Sho and learn what happened.

"Why don't we start from the top?" Norm said. "From the time of the accident. How were you able to disappear afterward?"

"I bribed the EMT drivers to let Mimi and me out near the hospital. I knew the accident was planned because my techs had checked all the equipment ten minutes before I was lowered, and it was perfect. That's why I was suspicious.

"Mimi led me through the mangroves to a small shack that looked no larger than a large storage shed, telling me it was the perfect hiding place. It was off the road, down a barely visible path, and covered by banyan branches. When we finally did find the shack, Mimi brought me in, sat me down, and lit a few candles so we could see. I soon understood Mimi wasn't hiding me. She planned on killing me."

"Why would she want to do that?" I asked.

"After Mimi left me in the shack, even though I was shaken up, I realized there was a hit out on me and Matt."

"Did you know who put one out on you?"

"Mercado never told me that Moss and he were lovers, but I knew Mercado well enough to figure it out. When Moss discovered Mercado and I were once partners, he assumed Mercado had told me about their affair and I'd expose him. Moss hired Mimi to carry out my execution. I would never have used the information against Moss, but he was much too paranoid to think I wouldn't."

"I attacked Mimi and put up a good fight, scratching and biting her until Mimi overwhelmed me. She tied me to the bed, and left, planning to return the next day to finish me off. She had to get back to the club to be seen, an alibi she desperately needed."

"Why would Moss use Mimi?"

"Mimi longed to be the ruling monarch of the queens in Key West, and I had always been in her way. Moss made Mimi a cash offer she couldn't resist. It was a two-fer and she loved bargains.

"When I awoke, I knew I had to escape before Mimi returned. I worked the knots until I had one hand free and then used it to untie the other. It took me most of the night, but I was able to free myself. I decided to wait until daylight for my next move. I needed to rest before my escape."

"You must have been exhausted and in shock," I said.

"I was but my outrage kept me going. I left the shack and started working my way through the thick brush, hoping to find safety. I swore I would survive, if for no other reason than to make sure Matt would be safe. By dusk, my clothes tattered and torn, feeling dehydrated and nearly delirious, I saw a clearing and made my way toward the light."

"Did you have any idea where you were?"

"None. I felt I had traveled miles, but in my state everything was disproportionate. I had been walking in circles. I emerged out of the brush into the parking lot of the hospital, only a mile from the shack. I wished I could have just walked in and found Matt and have been by his side, but that would have risked his life even more. I lay down next to a thicket, completely exhausted, and planned to rest for only a few minutes. I woke two hours later just in time to see Mercado pull into the parking lot. I used what remaining energy I had to drag myself out and get his attention. He ran to me and scooped me up."

"Did you tell him what happened?" I asked.

"I tried but he told me to save my strength. I could tell he was angry."

Norm looked at me and we were both thinking this was the trigger that caused Mercado to go after Moss.

"He brought me into the hospital through a back entrance and carried me to a utility room. He treated my severe dehydration by setting up an IV and cleaned many of my cuts and abrasions.

When he was able to get free, he brought his car close to the exit, transferred me to his car, and under the veil of night, took me to his home, where he knew I would be safe."

"That was kind of him," Norm said.

"He continued to care for me until he came up with the plan to move Matt by the hospital's helicopter. When that was in place, he made sure I could be included in the getaway. With the help of a few friends, Mercado had us flown to a private airfield near Miami and then transferred to the safe house of a family he knew in Coral Gables. And that's where we remained until it was safe to come back."

"You were really brave," Norm said.

"Never underestimate the drive of a drag queen."

"Amen."

We wrapped it up and gave her our good wishes. I was glad I knew her and understood why the community loved her.

MERCADO'S STATEMENT corroborated Sho's.

Mercado had confessed that he had knocked Moss out by giving him a high dose of Clonazepam, which Moss took routinely for panic attacks. This allowed Mercado to set up a suicide by hanging on New Year's Day.

Mercado had been having an affair with Moss for over five years, and each year, Moss promised to leave his wife, but the promises were as empty as a wino's bottle. When Mercado learned that Moss had tried to do away with his dear friend, Sho, he decided he had had enough. Motivated by hatred and revenge, he killed Moss.

As far as Knowles, Baxter, and Turino were concerned, like most sociopaths, Mercado didn't show any remorse for his victims. It was just business to him. The victims had screwed up and for that they had to pay with their lives. Raphael was able to take Mercado in and get credit for the collar. The doctor was being held without bail on charges of multiple homicides, first degree, psych evaluation pending.

With Sho's testimony, Mercado's confession, and the DNA found on the scrap of Sho's dress discovered by Officer Brooks, Mimi would ultimately be convicted of kidnapping and malicious attempt and was sentenced to serve two years in a prison upstate. Rumor has it she will be producing a show entitled *Jailbait*.

41

THE BOURGEOIS PIG

I got a call from Raphael the next day, asking me to meet
him in a public place. He was clever in anticipating that I didn't
want to be alone with him. I refused to see him at first, since I
still felt hurt and vulnerable. He promised he just wanted to talk
and begged for just an hour. I was wondering why it took me so
long to realize that all Raphael wanted was sex. But I had chosen
to continue with him despite his flaws, even though I knew it was
self-destructive.

There weren't many private places in Key West. Everyone knew
everyone else, so we decided to drive to Marathon. We ate at the
Bourgeois Pig, a local restaurant that served good food at reason-
able prices. Even better, we could sit at a booth and have some
privacy.

"I know you thought I was a complete jerk last time we met at
Sandy's. For that, I'm sorry."

"Glad you recognized that."

"I was trying to scare you into leaving town, but you don't scare
easily."

"I scare. I just try not to show it and no way was I going to leave a case right in the middle of it, even it meant being fired."

"I didn't call your boss, Lieutenant Brodsky," he said, staring at a plate of fries, avoiding my eyes.

"That was a low blow."

"I was trying to get you out of here, if that means anything."

Having this meeting was making me anxious and I wasn't able to eat much of my burger. In the course of the hour, I had only had two bites with a few sips of iced tea. But I was glad we were meeting, in spite of the awkwardness.

"I want you to know I really care for you," he said.

"You have a strange way of showing it."

"I'm not good at intimacy."

"No comment."

"I'd like to keep seeing you."

"I'm returning to Chicago in a few days. Besides, what makes you think I want to see you?"

"I'd be shocked if you did. But I'm in love with you, Nick."

"Whoa, bullfrog. We've gone from maybe seeing you again to you're in love with me. That's a huge leap there."

"I know I don't deserve someone like you. You're honest, ethical, and the real deal."

I kept a poker face to see what he'd come up with next. He was a con artist, and I had to protect myself.

"I've thought about what you said about listening to my father's orders. You're right. I haven't been my own man, ever. He's got clout and everyone does what he says. I'm ready to tell him I'm going to quit and move. That's how serious I am."

"You may be serious, but that doesn't excuse your lack of ethics when it comes to police work," I responded.

"I know. I don't think I ever cared about ethics or even knew what they were until I met you. I'm begging you to give me another chance."

"I don't think you're going to change, Raphael."

"Please. Won't you at least think about it?"

He sounded like a naughty child begging for forgiveness. All I knew about him was that he was good in bed. I had withdrawn back into my shell, not wanting to be hurt.

"I'm going back to Chicago. But—and this is a big but—I do believe in 'never say never,' so I will think about it, under one condition."

"What's that?" he asked, his eyes as big as the plates in front of us.

"That you tell your father you're done taking orders and resign."

"I told you I would."

"You've told me a lot of things, Raphael. Unfortunately, many of them were lies. You'd need to find something else to do. You don't deserve to be the chief. Maybe it's the way things work here, but this place isn't like any other I know."

"You're right. I've never thought of leaving but I will for you."

"I'm not making any promises. Let me think about it, Raphael. We're both just a plane ride away."

He smiled and nodded, and, for the first time, his stiff demeanor cracked. I saw his lip tremble.

Was he sincere? I really wanted to believe him but felt all the next moves were in his court. It would take a lot for me to ever trust him again. I wondered about my own sanity for even thinking of being with him. My shrink once said, "People often get into relationships to work out something from their own past." I didn't believe it at the time, but I wondered what I was trying to work out with Raphael. Was it my path of self-destruction?

I kept my thoughts to myself, and we left it at that as we drove back in silence.

42

When I got to the house, Jojo was playing hide-and-seek with Nathan. My friend was happier than a kid at his own birthday party.

"She said yes."

"Who did?"

"Merlot. Merlot said yes. We're getting married," he blurted.

"Whoo-hoo. Where? When? Congratulations, Jojo."

"Saturday. She's talked to Sho, and we're going to have a double wedding! Since the accident interrupted everything, Sho and Matt are redoing their vows in celebration of surviving their ordeal. There's a parade set for six p.m. Saturday, with floats filled with dwarves from around the world. My team is working with the city to make it happen."

Jojo was so excited he could barely stop to take a breath. "I want you and Norm to be on the float with us. The city plans to do it up big. Tina's a lay minister and is going to marry us on the beach. It's going to take place at sunset with fireworks and a reception after."

"Jojo, that's great! I know you two will be very happy."

"Thanks. Merlot's met Nathan, and she wants to hold him instead of a bouquet."

"What about her dog, Gigi?"

"She's going to be ring bearer."

Nathan barked and looked up at me as if to say, "I can't wait."

I shook my head and said with total conviction, "Only in Key West."

IT WAS ONE OF THE MOST well-attended events in Key West, with worldwide publicity. Many politicians rode in the parade, but I was surprised to see Raphael in one car with a sign that said, "PEREZ FOR MAYOR." Vladimir sat in the car with him. He was running for sheriff. My interest in ever seeing Raphael again plummeted instantly, and I was fine with that.

I just stood watching, surprised but not shocked. I wondered if in time he might run for president.

ACKNOWLEDGMENTS

I'm very thankful to Gary Marion and all of the other entertainers at 801 Bourbon Bar, who not only let me sit in on their staff meetings and watch their shows, but also invited me backstage to observe as they transformed from extraordinary men to beautiful women. Their interactions with the audience revealed insights into their unique method of teaching the acceptance of differences.

Through ride-alongs, interviews, and procedures, which were all invaluable, the Key West and Miami police departments afforded me a firsthand glimpse of the services they provide.

Special thanks to my friends and families (biologically determined in Detroit and chosen in Key West), who offered support and guidance. Thanks to Mark Bormes, who supplied honest opinions, whether I liked them or not.

My gratitude to my dream team of developmental/copy editor Alan Rinzler, who kept me on the straight and narrow by insisting on an outline and structure; Claire Petrie, copy editor and proofreader, who gave me invaluable perspectives, and kept wondering if I had started my third book; and Diane Aronson, copy editor/production editor and all-around support person, who worked, regardless of her unwieldy schedule, into the wee hours. To round out the editorial team, Lisa Mahoney, who served as copy editor

ACKNOWLEDGMENTS

on the second round, sharing invaluable observations, and Susan Groarke and Sandra Smith, exceptional proofreaders.

Laura Duffy came up with a creative cover, one that captures the old and the new Key West, which continually evolves, while Karen Minster designed the interior, which keeps the continuity of *The Gay Detective* while assimilating elements of contemporary society, a feat unto itself. Sean Michaels designed my website, www .kennethdmichaels.com, which is a virtual-reality phenomenon.

Thank you to my early readers, Lynne Flanagan, Pati Weinhofer, Edgardo Alvarado-Vasquez, and the Key West Writers Guild, for their honest and invaluable feedback.

And, of course, Nathan the pug, who continues to sleep through my frustrations and gives me sympathetic stares when I'm blocked, a ruse to get more treats. Regardless, I appreciate his unconditional love and comedic antics. My readers no doubt realize I've paid Nathan my highest compliment by sharing him with Nick and Norm, now that they're proud pet parents.

A special thanks to Lorie Welsh, my personal assistant and side-kick, who consistently keeps me authentic, offers invaluable help, and delivers creative marketing nonpareil.

Thank you, readers, for your support and encouragement to continue this series.

If you enjoyed this book,
please leave a review
on Amazon or Goodreads.

———

I can be reached at
kenneth.michaels03@gmail.com
or through my website,
www.kennethdmichaels.com.

Chicago police detectives Nick Scott and Norm Malone are used to tracking down serial killers, not the other way around.

But then The Reaper has different plans.

Don't miss the first book in the Gay Detective series!

"As Nick and Norm close in on a surprise suspect, the pages practically turn themselves. Bodies keep piling up and things keep getting worse for Detective Scott, but readers will smile (and shiver) right to the end." —*Kirkus Reviews*

"I had a grand time reading *The Gay Detective* and am looking forward to reading the second book in the series, *Only in Key West*. This offbeat and marvelous police procedural has heart and humor tied up in a neat and well-written little package, and it's most highly recommended." —Jack Magnus, Readers' Favorite Book Reviews

"*The Gay Detective* by Kenneth D. Michaels is a well-written, suspenseful mystery." —Paige Lovitt, Reader Views Review

"Love this book. A perfect read for my trip to Key West. Interesting characters, nice pace of action and fun plot. Highly recommended." —Gary Ujifusa, Goodreads Review

CPSIA information can be obtained
at www.ICGtesting.com
Printed in the USA
LVOW12s2309040917

547547LV00001B/108/P